VENANDI

KC LUCK

FOREWORD

Thank you for your interest in *Venandi*. I sincerely hope you enjoy the story. It was a pleasure to write. If you find time, a review, or even better, a referral to another reader, is always appreciated.

Please enjoy!

KC

1

NEW ORLEANS, 1850

"Have you ever seen so many people in one place?" Willie asked as he stared around wide-eyed at the throngs of people filling Canal Street. Saxon hadn't and frankly, she wasn't sure she liked it. Willie and her other brother, Sam, talked her into coming with them to New Orleans for New Year's Eve. Going had been the topic of conversation for a month. When she hesitated, the two playfully ganged up on her.

"It's a new decade, Sax," Sam explained, grabbing her by the strap of her denim overalls and giving her a playful shake. He was two years younger but a head taller than she was at her five foot seven.

She slapped his hand away. "I'm well aware what year it is," she said, stern but with a smile. Ever since their mother died ten years before, she had raised the two boys. Of course, that didn't mean she was off the hook from working their small tobacco farm twelve hours every day, hence the overalls rather than the customary dress. Saxon didn't mind. Wearing men's clothing was her preference, and for the most part, she let everyone assume she was a man. All she had to do was hide her long, thick braid of brown hair under her felt hat, and passing was easy. She liked other things about being mistaken for a male, but those thoughts confused her a little. Unlike most women her age, marrying was not on her agenda. Men did not appeal to her. Women, however...

"Think of the party everyone will be having," Willie added to the argument. "We never go anywhere, and I'm itching to see what a real city is like." For Saxon, the idea was attractive. Although she was twenty-one, she'd never visited the booming city to the south either but heard stories regularly about how the place was the most exciting location anywhere. Some bragged even fancier now than Paris. Even though she resisted, a part of her was just as excited as her brothers. Seeing something different than plain old Prairieville at least once in her life seemed reasonable.

It didn't help that the three siblings had money in their pockets. Their father didn't often give them much when they sold a crop, but it had been a very successful season. In the end, Saxon relented, which was why the three stood with a mass of people, all shuffling toward the riverfront, in anticipation of a fireworks display. Apparently, this was only the third year of the spectacle, and excitement pulsed through the partygoers. The show would start any minute and ring in the new year. Jostled from all sides, Saxon was doubly glad she elected to stay dressed as a man. Willie and Sam didn't care, treating her more like a brother most of the time anyway. She certainly worked as hard as they did and never backed down from a rough and tumble with them.

Although she wore a simple sack coat and cotton breeches, other men wore everything from leather pants and drop sleeve work shirts to formalwear finished off with tall, shiny, black top hats. The ladies hanging on their arms flounced along in hoop skirts, the fancier ones colorful and embellished with ribbons and bows. Saxon often found her eyes wandering to some of the bolder women's drop shoulder sleeves and low necklines. There was nothing like that in Prairieville, and the stirring she felt low in her body both surprised her and made her curious. The desire to touch that fair skin with her fingertips continued to flash through her mind, and when a surge in the crowd pushed her closer to a beautiful, young, blonde woman, Saxon's heart quickened. There was no mistaking the feelings of want building up inside her. As she considered letting herself stumble even closer, there was a sudden presence beside her. "She's really quite beautiful, isn't she?" a woman's voice whispered in her ear.

Saxon jerked back, turning to look into the face of a woman so beautiful, it took her breath away. Green eyes accented a face of fair skin with full, red lips turned up in the hint of a smile and seem to match the burgundy-red, velvet dress she wore. Black hair cascaded in ringlets past her bare shoulders, barely captured under the smart matching bonnet on her head.

"What?" was all Saxon could manage to say, and the woman chuckled.

"Don't worry, your secret is safe with me," she answered in a voice pitched low and throaty. The sensualness of the sound rolled over Saxon, and again she was captivated. The stranger let her eyes drift up and down Saxon's body, and the smile widened a little. "All your secrets, darling."

A blush crept up Saxon's cheeks as she realized the woman knew exactly what she was and how she was feeling. "I don't—" she started, but then as swiftly as she arrived, the stranger slipped away into the crowd. Blinking, unsure if the woman was an apparition of her overstimulated imagina-

3

tion, Saxon looked around, noticing neither of her brothers were with her. Somehow, they had become separated, and anxiety clenched her stomach. The boys were a bit reckless by nature, and who knew what they would get mixed up in tonight. She needed to find them and pushed back through the crowd calling their names. As the fireworks began, progress was almost impossible as the tide of people nearing the riverfront carried her faster in their excitement. Only by elbowing her way did she break free of the mass to be spit out into a side alley.

The backsides of a row of three-story buildings boxed her in on both sides, making the space dark and hard to see. Her nose told her there were piles of trash lining the walls of the narrow space, and she stepped carefully as she moved in deeper. "Willie?" she called, knowing it was unlikely they were in there but hoping. "Sam?" There was no answer. In fact, it seemed she was completely alone. Frustrated, she turned to go back into the crowd when the sound of a footfall in the blackness at the end of the alley made her pause.

"What have we here?" a man's voice sounded from the dark. It was smooth but somehow disturbing at the same time. Saxon felt a trickle of fear run down her spine. "Lost, my young friend?" Every instinct in her wanted her to flee, but something about the voice kept her rooted in place. As she watched, a shadowy figure emerged into the faint bit of moonlight. He was tall, and dressed in elegant clothes, including a top hat. Somehow, that relaxed her more. He could not be some thug planning to roll her for the money in her pocket—just someone trying to be helpful.

"I'm looking for my brothers," she replied. "Two big farm boys." She waved in the direction of the crowd passing by, oblivious to the pair in the dark alley. "Out there somewhere, and I need to find them before they get into trouble."

The stranger walked closer, and even though she could see the lower half of his face, the brim of the top hat hid his eyes. "Trouble," he said, repeating her last word. "Yes, there's plenty of that to be had here." Saxon swallowed hard and wanted to back away but somehow couldn't. It was as if the man hypnotized her. "You've found a bit of it yourself, I'd say." With that, he smiled, and in the dark, his white teeth gleamed. Saxon's eyes widened as she thought for a moment she saw fangs. Her mind had to be playing tricks on her, because she was sure his eyes glowed red in the shadow. A part of her knew that was impossible and she should run, but another part wanted to wait. Wanted to see what the stranger was going to do next.

"That's enough, Andrew," someone said behind her, breaking the spell. Saxon recognized the voice. The sound was the beautiful woman in the burgundy-red hat who spoke to her in the crowd earlier. "She's with me." Saxon felt a cool hand slide along her arm, up to her shoulder to take hold. The grip was surprisingly strong, but the sensation of the woman's touch sent a shiver of excitement through her.

The man gave a little bow. "My apologies, Susan. I was not aware," he said and then backed away. "Enjoy your evening."

Only after he disappeared did Susan's grip lighten. She gently turned Saxon to face her, and like the last time, the woman's beauty captivated Saxon. Her eyes roamed over Saxon's face, and a mixture of emotions seemed to play in them. Saxon was sure there was a hint of sadness, or maybe regret, but more than anything, there was desire. A throb ran through her at the idea this sensual woman could want her so much.

The hand on her shoulder moved to touch her cheek, and what once felt cold seemed to burn Saxon's skin. Susan leaned in closer until their mouths were an inch apart. "Do you want to come home with me?" Susan whispered. Saxon did. She would find her brothers on the road home in the morning. After all, they were grown men and together could fend for themselves.

"Yes," she said, her voice breathless, and let Susan take her hand to lead her through the alley away from the masses. After a few twists and turns through the nearly empty streets of the French Quarter, they came to an opulent, three-story Creole townhouse tucked into a row of others with a similar design. All had round, white columns accenting tall, narrow porches. Open galleries wrapped in black wrought iron spread the width of the second and third floors. Black shutters framed each window, and in the center of it all was a white front door. Susan paused at its threshold, her hand on the door handle.

Her eyes met Saxon's and held. The greenness of her gaze seemed to deepen as she watched, and Saxon trembled with anticipation. "Are you sure you want to come in?" the woman asked, her voice like silk. Saxon licked her lips. She was never surer of anything as every part of her throbbed at the idea of being alone with this stranger.

"I am sure," she gasped, and Susan opened the door to let them inside.

2

LOS ANGELES, PRESENT DAY

S axon Montague took a deep breath and focused on Los Angeles' downtown skyline as the evening sank into twilight. It was a perfect November night with a touch of a cool breeze in the air. She enjoyed the feel of it across her cheeks, glad she'd put on her lightweight, black blazer to go with her designer jeans. She sat poolside listening to her manager explain yet again the specifics of Saxon's contract. The woman's name was Courtney Mason. She was new to the job but showed good instincts and came recommended by a longtime acquaintance who was already in the movie business. To be fair, Saxon was new to the industry too. Having directed only two movies to date, her peers called her a novice. Considering both films turned out to be block-buster thrillers, which also garnered some critical acclaim, everyone was suddenly paying attention. Everyone wanted a piece of her too.

"Saxon, are you listening?" Courtney asked, leaning forward in her gray business suit. Although Saxon knew she was on her side in the argument, a hint of exasperation was evident in her voice. "This is serious."

Not too sure she agreed about the importance of any of it, Saxon sighed and returned her focus to the conversation at hand. Her eyes fell on the movie executive who sat to her manager's left. Even though he had dressed casually in a yellow, short sleeve shirt and jeans, he was a powerful player. She knew the production company wasn't screwing around if they enlisted his help in making sure Saxon cooperated. In fact, they were sitting on the man's giant, outdoor patio drinking his expensive scotch. When he extended an invitation to meet personally, Saxon thought Courtney would hyperventilate at the news. Thankfully, she was acting calm and professional tonight.

With a sigh, Saxon set her crystal tumbler on the clear glass patio table between them. "I am listening," she said. "And I respect the seriousness of the conversation. However..." She paused, trying to come up with the right words to express how much she hated the idea of the next project. "No disrespect, but I am not the right choice for the movie you want me to direct."

"Why?" the movie executive asked. "You've made your name with the dark stuff. Hell, the tabloids can't get enough of how you've managed to bring back the old school feel of film noir." He shook his bald head, and Saxon believed he really was confused. She got that. A big-budget thriller with an edge of horror would be a film she would seem perfect for under normal circumstances.

Saxon caught the man's eye and held his stare. "I'm telling you, it's just not a good fit," she murmured. At first, the movie producer's eyes widened, but then he returned her look. She respected that. Most people would glance away in an instant, sensing something disturbing they would never be able to explain, but the executive producer did not. In a second, she knew he was a predator too, not in the sense of preying on eager young actors, but he loved the thrill of the kill-or-be-killed business of movies. He lived to win. That was why he would never let this go.

Feeling the tension in the air, Courtney cleared her throat. "Maybe we should talk about this in the morning. It's been a long day," she said, capping her Monte Blanc pen and preparing to stand. Saxon appreciated her manager's courage. This discussion was critical to her career too. If Saxon absolutely refused, they would both be blacklisted, yet she continued to fight on Saxon's behalf. The contract was simple but proving to be ironclad. Saxon, the up and coming red-hot movie director, was locked in a three-movie deal. So far, she'd directed two, and everyone made lots of money. Naturally, the production company expected her to do a third, and the budget set aside for the film was substantial. Saxon had every intention of fulfilling her obligation. Movie directing was interesting, a new challenge, and rather fun. Then, she read the movie script.

The executive dropped his stare to look at Courtney. Saxon knew he would; predator or not, he was no match for her, and if she had to guess, tonight he would have nightmares. "No," he said, a slight waver in his voice. He frowned and glanced in Saxon's direction again. She knew he was trying to figure out what he was feeling but then found his footing by going back to business. "We are already in preproduction, and money is being spent. Casting starts tomorrow morning. I want a commitment tonight."

Saxon saw Courtney look her way, a hint of pleading in her brown eyes. But only a hint, and again, Saxon felt impressed. It also meant she couldn't ruin her over this. No matter how much she hated the idea of taking the job. She even hated the name. *Venandi.* Her Latin was good enough to recognize the word's translation—hunter. Resigned, she gave the woman a small smile. "I'll do it," Saxon said. "But I want full control over who we cast as the lead."

Both Courtney and the executive producer let out a breath, their relief palatable. "Fine," the man said. "We are casting for the role tomorrow."

"You have a shot," Faye Stapleton heard her agent say over the phone. In her most comfortable sweats, she'd been pacing the perfectly decorated living room of her Beverly Hills home waiting for his call. "But I had to use some favors to get it." Faye closed her famous, hazel eyes and tried to contain her excitement over the news. Ever since she read the movie script her agent sent her last week, being the film's lead was all she could think about. At thirty-eight, her career was on the downslide, especially since her niche was the love interest in fun romcoms. Blonde, just the right amount of sexy, and charisma that jumped off the screen made her a perfect fit. The roles also made her rich, famous, and America's sweetheart, but never truly happy. With a degree from the California Institute of the Arts, Faye had expected to be cast in serious, complex roles that would impress the critics and get her nominated for awards. Her career had veered in a different direction from the start. Although she did not regret her decisions at the time, a part of her was not ready to give up on a chance to be the actress she dreamed of since she could remember. The role in this movie would be that opportunity.

"Thank you, Walt," she finally said. "Thank you, thank you, thank you. You have no idea what this means to me."

Walt chuckled. The sound suited him as he could easily be mistaken for Santa Claus on any given day. White beard, chubby belly and all, he was a well-respected veteran in the entertainment business, and Faye had been with him from the start. He was the one who steered her toward romantic comedies, and his instinct was spot on. She became a star because of his advice. Thankfully, he was willing to listen to what she needed to fulfill her dreams at this stage in her life. Hence his tracking down a part completely different than anything she ever considered. A part that could change the perception of her career and help her stay in the business. "Well, don't thank me too much," Walt said. "You're the last actress on the list of auditions. I actually talked them into adding the slot on the schedule just for you."

"I won't let you down," she said, trying to sound more confident than she felt. "I'll rehearse all night."

"Do that," Walt said. "Call me as soon as you finish tomorrow and nail this thing. I believe in you, kiddo." Before Faye could thank him again, he was gone. With a dozen other actors relying on him, she knew there were more calls he had to make that night. Setting down the phone on the end table, a wave of nerves washed over Faye as she considered his words. The opportunity really was a favor, and she was damn lucky to get it. This was not an audition she could screw up and considering she hadn't tried out for a role in over a decade, this would not be easy. Twisting her long, blonde hair into a messy bun, she picked up the script sitting beside her phone and got ready to start rehearsing. Before she made another move, her cellphone rang. Snatching the thing up, assuming the call was from Walt again, she didn't check the screen. She didn't manage to say hello before the breathing started. Deep, raspy, and menacing.

Faye felt the familiar trickle of fear at the sound. "Who is this?" she demanded, but like always, the caller didn't answer. Yanking the phone from her ear, she checked the screen, but it said 'Unknown Caller.'" Faye pressed the button to hang up and dropped the phone on the end table again. Nearly every night was the same. It was too much, and after her audition tomorrow, she would finally go to the police. Enough was enough.

Sliding her finger over the glossy surface of the pretty face of the latest actress' black and white headshot, Saxon worked hard to keep her irritation in check. Ten auditions took all the morning and part of the afternoon. A few bigger names, some new faces, but none had suited her—a waste of time. Today's outcome was just another red flag that *Venandi* would be a disaster for Saxon.

"I'm done," she said to the casting agent sitting beside her. Dropping the picture onto the table, she pushed back her chair to stand. "You need to go back to the drawing board. Find someone different. These aren't working."

The young man looked as frustrated as she did, and taking off his glasses, he leaned back in the folding chair. The casting agent obviously knew better than to come right out and say Saxon was being difficult. Still, his eyes couldn't hide what he was thinking. "We start shooting in less than two weeks," he advised, telling Saxon something she already knew. Her hesitancy to accept the project initially set her back on prep, and everyone felt the pressure. Still, the wrong actress in the lead would make an already unpleasant assignment unbearable.

"It's not unprecedented to start filming a movie without casting the lead actress," Saxon explained. "Selznick pulled it off in *Gone with the Wind*."

The casting agent gave Saxon a blank stare. "*Gone with the Wind*?" he finally mumbled. For a second, she was afraid he would say he never heard of the 1930s classic. Then, he shook his head. "You're younger than I am, but you know some random trivia. Where do you come up with all this stuff?"

Saxon shrugged. "I've watched a lot of movies," she said, standing. The answer was more than an understatement. "Let me know when you have more names."

"Wait," the man said, raising his hand. "There is one more. A late add."

Shaking her head, Saxon was not interested. She wasn't sure she could handle sitting through another reading. "No, thanks. I have an appointment."

As if he didn't hear her, the casting agent held out the actress's info sheet. "The executive producer added her himself. A favor to some old friend," he explained. "We need to get through this."

"Who the hell is it?" Saxon growled through gritted teeth, and the casting agent grinned, clearly taking pleasure in giving Saxon more bad news. She could tell he thought whoever the actress was, she would not be a good fit. Snapping the page from his hand, she looked to see the name. Faye Stapleton. The rom-com actress who was growing too old to last as America's sweetheart and play the cute girl next door. "Ridiculous," was all she could think to say.

The casting agent nodded. "We are in agreement on that one," he said. "But like I said, someone pulled strings to get her this." He handed her the woman's headshot. "We can make it short. Five minutes."

Saxon looked over the photo. A famous face and a decent actress in her opinion, but the range she was looking for just wasn't there. Still, there seemed no way out of it. "Call her in," she said and sat back down. "Let's get this over with."

3

Taking deep breaths to steady her nerves, Faye forced herself not to pace the empty, nondescript waiting room in the suite of Hollywood offices. One by one, the actresses left, and none returned. Some Faye was friends with, even worked on films with a couple of them while the others were quiet, and one or two even looked starstruck in her presence. One thing was clear though, all seemed surprised to see her there. Not only was she high enough in the Hollywood echelons to not need to audition with the masses, but the movie role was also far from anything she'd done in the past—a fact her subconscious kept trying to remind her. But she refused to listen. She wanted this role and didn't plan to leave the building until she gave everything she had to get it.

Suddenly, the door opened, and a production assistant stuck her head in. She was ridiculously young and bright-eyed, but Faye didn't hold that against her. No doubt the girl was new to the business, starting at the very bottom of the food chain, and everything was fresh and fun. Faye could remember that wonderful feeling of excitement, so she gave her a smile. "They are ready for you, Ms. Stapleton," she said and waited while Faye gathered her things before following her.

"Thank you," Faye said and had the urge to ask the girl if she knew how any of the others had done but restrained herself. Odds were the production assistant wouldn't know anything, and the question would make her seem desperate. Even if that was a little like how she was feeling, she didn't want anyone to know and, with that in mind, squared her shoulders to prepare for whatever happened next.

As they entered the soundstage, the production assistant gave Faye a smile. "Good luck," she said and then ducked out of the space. Faye stood alone under the lights. Blinking, she registered two people sitting at a table in the shadows. One had to be the casting agent, but the other could be anyone. Maybe another member of the casting crew, like a producer, even the director. She wondered for a moment if that was who sat there—Saxon Montague. They had never met, but everyone in Hollywood knew who she was and that she seemed to have the Midas touch. Ironically, the young director never allowed photographs, and so far, the paparazzi were unsuccessful in capturing her in a picture— a remarkable feat in this day and age. The fact did make her more mysterious, and Faye was curious to see what she looked like. Unfortunately, the bright white lights made it challenging to see anything behind them.

"Thank you for coming, Ms. Stapleton," one of the two silhouettes said. "I'm Mark, one of the casting agents on the picture."

Faye gave Mark her legendary smile. "It's my pleasure. I appreciate the opportunity." The casting agent cleared his throat, and Faye felt a sliver of uncertainty. The idea he might dismiss her without a reading crossed her mind. No doubt they had a long day and perhaps even someone in mind for the part. She was not going to let that happen. "Mark," she said, taking the initiative and dropping all essence of the girl-next-door persona that had made her famous. She was not going to let some casting agent ruin her chance at this role. "What scene did you want me to perform today?"

There was a pause. "Well, Ms. Stapleton, here's the thing..." Mark started, and Faye felt a wave of nausea roll in her stomach as she realized they really weren't going to let her audition. They were just doing the favor for Walt and nothing more. About to express her desire to perform the scene, she stopped when the second person at the table spoke.

"Scene nineteen, page forty-eight," the woman said. "You're speaking with the pathologist over the body of a victim, performing the role of an FBI profiler."

Faye nodded. "All right," she said, focusing all her attention on the woman at the edge of the light. No matter who she was, Faye knew a lifeline when someone threw her one. "Who will be reading the pathologist's lines?" She heard the two at the table whisper something back and forth for a second. There almost seemed to be a disagreement between them as to who would read. Normally, she would expect the casting agent to do the task, but it seemed the other person wanted the job.

"I will," the woman finally said. "Let me know when you are ready."

When the sound of Faye Stapleton entering the soundstage reached Saxon's ears, she wasn't paying much attention but instead reading the woman's credentials. Her experience was impressive, but it did not change the fact the actress was wrong for the part. *Venandi* was not going to be lighthearted, but dark, sinister, and unsettling. She had a tone in mind. If she could capture the essence of what Jonathan Demme did in *Silence of the Lambs*, the movie might be redeemable. Maybe. Yet, when the actress spoke, something underlying in her tone made Saxon raise her eyes. There was an edge there. A hunger. Intrigued, she looked past the glare of the light and was struck by the woman's beauty. Yet, there was more. Something in her stance drew Saxon in, and she understood why Faye Stapleton was so famous—she was compelling. Even dressed in a perfectly tailored, all-business black pantsuit, she radiated appeal. Her blonde hair pulled back, leaving her neck exposed, only added to her sensualness. It had been a long time since someone affected her that much, and Saxon knew the attraction was another reason the woman could not be in her movie.

Still, when the casting agent started to dismiss Faye, Saxon interrupted. She wasn't ready for the actress to leave yet. Even if she never saw her again, she wanted to enjoy the moment. Saxon could tell the casting agent was irritated by her sudden change of mind, but after a quick discussion, she got what she wanted.

Waiting, Faye turned her head to look into the shadows directly at Saxon. Her hazel eyes seemed to pierce the darkness beyond the light. This did nothing to diminish Saxon's desire, but she forced the feeling down determined to focus.

"I'm ready," Faye Stapleton said in answer to Saxon's instruction, catching her off guard. The actress did not seem to want to take a moment and refresh her mind about the scene from the script.

"You're sure?" Saxon asked, leaning forward to rest her forearms on the table. Most of the other actresses literally read the lines. She looked deep into Faye's eyes, knowing the actress could not see her. "It's understandable if you want to use the script."

Faye lifted her chin and did not drop her gaze. "Yes, I'm sure," she said, her voice firm. "I have the current version memorized." Saxon paused, taking in her answer. This was impressive, not just because she knew the script by heart, but because she was confident enough to keep looking straight into the darkness.

Even more captivated, Saxon tilted her head. "Fair enough," she said. "Put your things down and begin at the start of the scene." Without hesitation, Faye set her business bag aside and began. As Saxon watched, the woman's demeanor became even more confident, with a touch of clinical to make the role convincing. She did indeed know her lines, and even though there was no prop of a decimated dead body on an autopsy table, she seemed to somehow make it feel like there was one. Whenever Saxon spoke her part, the woman fixed her with the serious stare again. She exuded the expertise of a veteran FBI agent. As the two discussed the victim's horrible death, Saxon was entirely sucked into the scene. Faye's carefree, girl-next-door persona had vanished into the calculated and complex role of a profiler who specialized in capturing serial killers. There was no denying she was perfect.

Standing from the table, Saxon walked into the lights to finish the scene face to face. Faye didn't miss a beat, although Saxon sensed her heart beating faster at her approach. "And what was the ultimate cause of death?" Faye asked, saying her last line of the scene, holding Saxon's gaze as if she were only the pathologist and not someone who would decide her fate. Her tone did not waver and was the perfect blend of gravity and curiosity.

"Acute blood loss," Saxon answered. "Drained from the body."

When the scene ended, Faye simply stood still, continuing to look into the face of the woman who read lines with her. She didn't know exactly who she was yet, but if she were forced to guess, Faye would say she was Saxon Montague, the film's movie director and a rising star in the industry. She was noticeably younger than Faye expected with smooth, flawless fair skin and short, brown hair styled in a messy cut that suited her. Her eyes, though, were the thing that gave away a hint she was older than her appearance. They were a deep, dark brown, almost black against the bright light behind her, and seemed to hold the wisdom of the ages. Impossible, of course, Faye knew, but the thought lingered. Something else lingered too, and it took a moment for her to realize an undeniable attraction to Saxon. The sound of her voice as she read the lines, the way she stood with easy confidence, and the way her gaze lingered as if she was seeing into Faye's soul. She wasn't sure she liked the reaction yet didn't want the moment between them to end. All of which could spell nothing but a disaster.

Learning early on that movie industry relationships were fraught with pitfalls, Faye steered clear. She hardly dated at all, going out just enough to keep the paparazzi happy. There was occasional speculation she was interested in a male costar, but that would fade soon after the movie finished its box office run. There was another reason too—Faye preferred women, and the fact was her deep, dark secret. If news got out she was a lesbian, her career would be ruined, which was enough to keep Faye basically celibate. But somehow this was different. Faye was sure she'd never felt such a pull toward another human being. An instantaneous attraction, and Faye was certain she did not feel it alone. There was a hunger in Saxon's eyes as well.

"Okay," the casting agent said, coming onto the soundstage and breaking the spell. "Thank you for auditioning, Ms. Stapleton. We will be in touch with your agent soon." Pulling her eyes away from Saxon's face, Faye tried to compose herself. Her heart was racing, and she could feel a flush of heat climbing her neck. The reaction seemed ridiculous, but she couldn't seem to contain it.

Forcing herself to focus on the man trying to usher her along, Faye nodded. "I appreciate you taking the time to let me read," she said. "I'm very excited about this role."

"Of course," Mark replied. "Again, we will be in touch." Faye did not like the dismissive tone in his voice. It was frustrating. She knew she nailed the audition, but this was out of her control. There was nothing to do but wait.

"I want her," she heard Saxon say and turned to look at the movie director still standing in the same spot.

The casting agent held up his hands. "Wait, just hold on," he started. "We need to—"

Saxon shook her head, and resolve etched her face. Faye could see there would be no argument in the director's decision, and her heart soared. The woman wanted her, and she forced herself to ignore all that it could mean. "I want her," Saxon repeated. "And I'm not taking no for an answer." The woman let her eyes drift back to Faye's, and a smile played across her full, slightly parted lips. "She's convincing." Then she paused as if what she was about to say was most important of all. "As an FBI profiler using her profession to disguise that she is a vampire hunter."

4

As the sun set over the Pacific Ocean, Saxon wore dark sunglasses and watched it from the covered balcony of her Malibu beach house. Normally, this quiet moment between day and night relaxed her, but she was restless this evening. And she knew why. Faye Stapleton. This afternoon Saxon made a mistake and shook her head thinking about it. Casting Faye as the lead in *Venandi*, especially in the role of a vampire hunter of all things, was simply playing with fire. No one affected Saxon quite the way the hazel-eyed blonde actress had today, and she had let her most primal emotions control her. Something she rarely let happen. It wasn't smart and, regardless of the fact Faye nailed the audition, and she honestly had, putting her in the movie could be a disaster. When they had stood face to face on the soundstage after her reading, the air between them crackled with electricity. As attracted as Saxon was to the woman, she knew Faye felt the same pull by the way her body reacted. How her eyes dilated, her breath coming quicker, even the acceleration of her heartbeat, they all gave her away. Saxon's overly keen senses missed none of the signals.

All of which only made things worse, and as Saxon played with the glass of expensive Bordeaux on the small table beside her, she knew what she must do. She needed to insist the production company let her leave the picture. Her instincts had been right all along. A movie about a vampire being profiled as a serial killer was terrible. The fact he was hunted down after leaving a trail of victims was the last thing she should be involved in. The irony was almost laughable. And yet, a part of her fought against the decision to quit. Not only did she give her word last night, but her manager, Courtney, would pay the highest price. It would probably ruin her career in Hollywood. As would Saxon's most likely, but really it didn't matter. She moved from job to job when she wanted or sometimes would go years with doing nothing at all. Time was irrelevant.

The sound of a sliding glass door opening made Saxon turn her head to look. A tall, distinguished, older gentleman stood there. "Good evening," he said, and Saxon smiled. Her assistant Louis had arrived home at last. He would have good advice about how she should handle the situation.

"Good evening," she said. "Bad traffic?"

The man sighed. "Isn't there always?" he answered, a hint of a Georgia accent in his voice. "I don't know why you picked Los Angeles this time. Nashville was so much more charming."

Saxon agreed. Nashville had been fun, and so was the country music industry, but she could only stay in one place and one role for so long. At best, she could manage a decade, maybe a little longer, before people started to notice she was different. Little things like never aging couldn't be overlooked forever. Of course, Louis knew the reasons they had to leave, but he never liked changes. Even after fifty-three years of service.

Saxon smiled. "Thank you for going," she said. "Any problems?"

"None," he replied. "Would you like me to prepare something for you?" Saxon considered his question and assessed how she felt. Her energy was adequate although she hadn't taken in nourishment in a while. Part of the reason was because of her excitement over Faye Stapleton. The actress energized her. The attraction made her feel alive.

"Not just yet." She motioned toward the second chair on the balcony. "Join me. I need your advice."

Louis gave her a little bow and slid gracefully into the seat. Everything about Louis was charm and sophistication. People would be surprised to learn of his past and how Saxon found him broken from abuse and starving on the streets of Atlanta when he was just a boy of eleven. Abandoned by his mother and never knowing his father, he was left to fend for himself in the gutters of the large city. If not for Saxon, Louis would not have lived long. A gentle boy by nature, he did not have the killer instincts necessary to survive. When Saxon happened across him, Louis was in a dark alley cornered by two older boys who wanted unspeakable things from him. After Saxon scared them off, Louis begged for her protection and, in exchange, agreed to serve her. Over the years, she trained him on what she needed, and the arrangement proved to be a good one. Saxon had come to rely on him as more than a servant but as a confidant and a friend. Sitting on the deck, he looked at her, his eyes appraising. "Now you have made me curious. Clearly, something is bothering you tonight," he said. "But I can't tell if it is good or bad."

Saxon sighed. "That is my problem as well. I can't decide either," she said. "But... I've met someone."

Louis' eyebrows went up. "Someone?" he asked. "A

woman perhaps?" Saxon nodded, although Faye was so much more than just a woman. She radiated charisma, energy, and for lack of a better word, life. Studying Saxon, Louis didn't say anything for a moment. Glancing at him, Saxon was glad to see there was no judgment in his eyes. Only compassion. "Do you want her?"

Saxon paused, truly examining her feelings. "I do," she finally answered. "Like I haven't in I can't remember how long." Neither said anything for a few minutes and instead studied the darkness over the ocean.

"Who is she?" Louis asked, and Saxon snorted a derisive laugh. The answer could not be worse.

"I cast her as the lead in the vampire movie," she murmured, and Louis turned to stare at her. He didn't need to say how dangerous the situation was, but she wanted his input. "Tell me I should walk away, Louis."

Again, the man paused and then sighed. "Saxon, this will be hard for you, but it's time you follow your heart again. You've waited long enough."

"You got it? Oh my God," Faye's best friend squealed. They were sitting in Faye's grand kitchen. With appliances that were professional chef grade and everything in shades of gray and white with black accents, the space had been featured in an interior design magazine last spring. The two women sat with glasses of pinot noir at the eight-foot-wide marble island and talked about Faye's day. "When you sent me that vague text, I thought I was coming over to console you. This is amazing."

Faye grinned over the rim of her wine glass. The news was indeed amazing, and she still had to pinch herself at times to believe it happened. She was cast as the lead in what could easily be the next thriller blockbuster. Here was her chance to take her career in a different direction. "I wanted to tell you in person," Faye said to her friend. She and Jane Hanover had been close since they worked on Faye's first romantic comedy. Jane played the comical side-kick, but soon after gave up on the industry. She decided to become a mom and married an LAPD cop who absolutely doted on her. Their two red-headed boys were holy terrors but at the same time adorable too. Faye was their godmother and loved them with all her heart.

Sobering a little, Jane reached out and put her hand on Faye's forearm. "I'm so happy for you, Faye," she said. "I know you wanted this more than anything." Then, the bubbly friend was back and nearly bouncing in her chair. "Did you meet Saxon Montague? Is she scarred? I think that's why she won't pose for photographs."

Faye laughed. "She's most definitely not. The woman is, well..." she paused, feeling a blush creep up her neck, unable to think of how best to describe the mysterious, sensual persona that made up Saxon Montague. A glance at Jane and she saw her friend's mouth was open in surprise.

"Faye Stapleton, are you crushing on her?" she asked, and Faye adamantly shook her head.

"No," she said, trying to hide how attracted she was to the movie director. "She's just really different. Interesting, you know?"

Jane sipped her wine while keeping a critical eye on her best friend. Faye could tell she wasn't buying her story. The few incredibly discreet hook-ups with other secret lesbian actresses were always dissected at length after. None of the relationships lasted more than a few weeks, and so far, Jane was not impressed with any of them. There was never one like Saxon though. "Is she sexy?" Jane finally asked as she set down her glass.

Faye could not contain her grin. "Like no one I've ever met. Her sex appeal almost made me dizzy."

Jane's eyes widened. "How close to her did you get?" she asked, and Faye explained about the reading.

"And at the end, while we were staring into each other's eyes and the casting agent was trying to dismiss me..." she let her voice drift off.

"What?" Jane asked as if she was ready to explode. "Don't hold out on me."

Faye remembered the moment and felt a wave of heat rise from her center. Unable to help it, she licked her lips. "She said she wanted me," she whispered. "I almost melted on the spot."

Jane gasped. "Oh honey, this is so not good," she said. "She might not even be a lesbian." Faye started to agree when there was a buzz at her gate. Not expecting anyone, she furrowed her brow.

"That's weird," she said and went to the intercom to ask who it was ringing.

"FedEx, ma'am," came the voice over the speaker. That was even more unusual. Packages and other mail always went through her manager's office. She never received things at her private residence.

Not sure what to do, she pressed the button again. "Do you mind telling me who it is from?" she asked. There was a pause, and she imagined the driver was looking through his pile for her individual package.

"It's from Entity Realty in Tahoe City, Nevada," he finally said, and Faye tilted her head. That sounded harmless enough. She pushed the button to open the gate.

"Buying another place?" Jane asked, and she shook her

head. She was raised and graduated from high school in Tahoe City, Nevada. A childhood spent skiing the slopes at Heavenly Mountain every winter and jet skiing on Lake Tahoe in the summer was a good one. She tried to visit her parents a couple times a year but had no plans to move back there anytime soon.

Going to the door, she opened it to watch the familiar green, white, and purple colored FedEx truck pull up. The driver hopped out and approached with a long narrow box. He was blushing a little, and when he got close, Faye knew what was about to come next. She was well acquainted with the overwhelmed look of a fan meeting her in person. "Ms. Stapleton, I'm a big fan. My wife will die when she hears I met you tonight," he said. "Could I maybe have an auto-graph?" He held out a blank FedEx form and a pen.

Faye gave him her famous smile. "Of course. What's your wife's name?" she asked, and when he responded it was Vivian, Faye quickly scribbled a 'thank you for being a fan' note on the form and signed it.

"Thank you so much," he gushed as he backed away, almost shaking with excitement. "She really will go crazy over this." Faye gave him a little wave as he turned around and drove back down her driveway. She looked at the package. Like the driver said, the return address was Tahoe City, but she had never heard of the realty office. Going back inside, Jane was waiting at the island having poured them more wine.

"Well?" she asked. "What is it?" Faye set the box on the countertop and opened the package. What she saw inside made her heart jump into her throat. There were three long stem roses. Red buds, but instead of being beautiful, they were dead, shriveled, and ugly.

5

NEW ORLEANS, 1850

Taking Saxon's hand, Susan led her into the townhouse. Although Susan's skin was cool under her fingertips, at the contact, Saxon almost flinched. The touch was so electric. The desire she already felt bloomed hotter, and Saxon licked her lips. As if sensing the change, Susan turned and let her green eyes roam her face. Longing smoldered in the look, and a tightness formed low on Saxon's body. An ache. She had no experience with women, or anyone, not even a kiss, and she did not know what to do but sensed Susan planned to teach her. As if reading her mind, the woman raised their joined hands and opened Saxon's before bringing it to her face to caress her cheek. Saxon shivered, amazed something so simple could be so erotic. Susan leaned into the touch, closing her eyes. "Thank you for coming in," she said, her gentle voice laced with genuineness. "This means more to me than you can possibly know."

"I want this," was all Saxon could manage to gasp as her heart raced. She desperately needed to please her—to take her in her arms, to kiss her, and to do things she could barely imagine. Stepping closer, she slipped her hand to the back of Susan's neck and closed her eyes before leaning in to find her mouth. For a moment, she thought she could feel the brush of Susan's lips, but then Susan stepped back.

"Not yet," she murmured, turning her back to a confused Saxon. After a pause, as if gathering herself, Susan glanced over her shoulder. "Let's share a moment in the parlor first."

She led Saxon to a room just off the hall. As they entered, Saxon had never seen a space so lavish and charming. She stopped in the doorway and took in everything, knowing she would probably never again be in a room like that one. There was no one in Prairieville with a house grand enough to even have a parlor. A whitewashed brick fireplace was centered on the far wall with the portrait of a woman in a gilded frame above it. The dark wood floor, polished to a gleam, was partially covered with an area rug of deep red and gold swirls. Clearly seeing the wonder on Saxon's face, Susan smiled and waved toward one of the room's matching gold velvet sofas. "Please, sit down," she said as she moved to the sideboard. "Let me make something for us."

Perched on the edge of the sofa, Saxon watched in the warm glow of the hanging oil lamps as the woman poured a vibrant green liquid into two small, delicate glasses. With a practiced hand, she used tongs to place a cube of sugar on a gold, slotted spoon she held over one of the glasses. Slowly, she dripped water over the sugar until it melted into the drink. The liquid grew cloudy yet seemed to glow in the lamp light. Like everything else that night, the drink was exotic and intrigued her. "That's beautiful," she said. "What is it?"

Finishing the second glass, Susan picked them up and turned to her. Saxon noticed the green of the drink almost matched her eyes. "This is absinthe," she explained. "A special treat for us to enjoy tonight. After all, it is a new year." She handed one of the small, delicate glasses to Saxon. "I think you will like it."

Never doubting anything the woman said, Saxon took one of the drinks from her and, following Susan's lead, took a sip. The taste of black licorice slid over her tongue, and she savored the flavor. Liking the taste, she took another swallow, and after a moment, a feeling of warmth bloomed in her belly. Her craving for Susan only heightened as the alcohol relaxed her inhibitions, and a throb started between her legs. She let out a wavering breath. "I do like it," she said. "Very much."

Susan smiled. "I'm so glad," she said and drank her own glassful. Once it was empty, she licked her red lips before setting the glass down. "Now, if you'll excuse me, I need to go upstairs. This won't take long. Will you wait?" Saxon nodded. Mesmerized by her, she knew she might wait forever if she asked.

"Yes," she answered. "I'll be right here."

"Thank you," Susan said as she breezed out of the parlor, leaving Saxon alone.

She let her eyes drift over the objects in the room until they landed on the portrait above the fireplace mantle. The painting was of a striking young woman in what looked to her like a royal blue ball gown. Her eyes seemed to match the color of the dress, and the painter had captured a hint of a smile on her pink lips. Blonde hair was pinned up with only a few tendrils hanging loose to frame her delicate neck. Intrigued, Saxon stood to move closer. There was something about the woman's face that drew her in, and as she studied the portrait, Saxon has the strongest desire to touch the painting. She wanted to trace her finger along those slightly parted lips. They were sensual as if the artist captured more than her likeness, but part of her soul.

Raising her hand as if she were in a trance, Saxon was about to caress the painting when she heard someone behind her. Caught doing something she shouldn't, she dropped her hand and turned to see Susan. She had changed her clothes. No longer in the burgundy velvet evening dress, she wore a graceful, black silk robe. Letting her eyes drift to the gap at the neckline, Saxon felt her breath come quicker. The smooth, pale skin showing a hint of the woman's breast looked so tempting. The craving to put her mouth there, to trail kisses along the curve and go lower, made her dizzy. "She's really quite beautiful, isn't she?" Susan asked, a hint of a smile playing across her lips, no doubt appreciating Saxon's reaction to her change of attire. Saxon blinked, confused for a moment, and then realized she spoke of the portrait.

Turning back to look at the image of the young woman, Saxon nodded. "Very," she said. "Who is she?" Susan stepped closer, and their shoulders brushed, making Saxon suck in a breath. The contact was electrifying and threatened to overwhelm her senses. Again, her eyes drifted to the hint of Susan's partially exposed breasts, and she licked her lips.

Clearly sensing her reaction, Susan leaned into her, letting her body press against Saxon's for a moment. Unable to control her response, Saxon moaned and reached for her waist, wanting to pull her in tighter, but then the woman withdrew with a low chuckle. "Patience," she whispered. "Everything will be worth the wait." Then, she returned her attention to the portrait. "Her name was Katherine."

"Katherine," Saxon repeated and once again felt the pull of the painting. "The name suits her."

Susan sighed, a manner of sadness coming over her. "Yes. She was incredibly special to me," she said with a wistfulness in her voice. "I miss her every day." Unsure if she should pry, Saxon stayed quiet, and after a long moment, Susan turned from the painting. She met Saxon's eyes, and her red lips pulled into a smile. "But now you are here to keep me company."

Liking the sound of the words, Saxon nodded. "I am," she replied. "All for you."

"All for me," Susan repeated in a whisper. "Then let's not keep you waiting." Running her hands up Saxon's arms, strong from lifting bales of tobacco, she stepped closer. Her body grazed Saxon's, driving her wild with want.

"I want to kiss you," Saxon said, her voice breathless. "I need to."

Susan's eyes widened, and she could see her own hunger reflected in them. She leaned in until their lips were almost touching. Saxon shivered. "Then, kiss me," Susan said, and unable to restrain herself any longer, she did. The feel of their mouths coming together sent a surge of passion through Saxon, straight to her core. Even in her imagination, when she wondered what a kiss might feel like, there was no comparison to the power of that moment. A moan came from deep in her throat, and slipping her hands around Susan's waist, she pulled her in tighter. Their bodies pressed together while their tongues touched. On instinct, as Susan parted her lips wider in invitation, Saxon took the kiss deeper, ravishing Susan's mouth with all the hunger she felt pent up inside her.

All those times late at night back on the farm, when everyone else was asleep, Saxon fantasized what a woman might feel like naked beneath her. The nights when she let her hands drift down her stomach until she felt the wetness between her legs. An ache always built inside her, yet she never found a way to release the feelings. She had the same ache for Susan and wondered if the woman would be wet like she knew she was at this moment. The strongest yearning to find out made her break the kiss and rest her forehead against Susan's. "I want more," she gasped and felt Susan nod.

"There will be more," she promised. "Much, much more. But first, I want you to come with me."

Conflicted, wanting to push the woman back onto the sofa and see what she wore beneath the robe raged inside her. Still, the desire to obey Susan's wishes was equally strong. As if sensing the internal conflict, Susan pulled away with a small smile playing across her lips. "We have all the time in the world, darling." Once again, she took Saxon's hand and led her. Leaving the parlor, they walked down the hall until they reached a closed door. A woman stood beside it, dressed in the black dress and white apron of a house servant. Saxon was surprised there was someone else in the house with them so late into the night but knew she had no experience with life in the city. Susan's world could not be more different than her own.

"Everything is as you requested, ma'am," the servant said with her eyes lowered. "Do you need anything else?"

Susan smiled at the woman. "Nothing more," she said. "You may go." Then, as if it was an afterthought, she said. "And Happy New Year."

The servant nodded, keeping her eyes lowered. "Thank you, ma'am. Happy New Year," she said and then hurried away. As she left, Susan opened the tall, wooden door so Saxon could see the space was a washroom, yet unlike any she had seen before. Like the parlor, it was lavish, and a large, white, clawfoot bathtub stood in the middle. Steam rose from the water inside. Saxon furrowed her brow, not understanding, but followed willingly as Susan stepped in before stopping to close the door. Releasing her hand, Saxon watched as Susan unfastened the one button of her sack coat.

"Let's take this off," she said, pushing the fabric from Saxon's shoulders and letting it fall to the floor before reaching for the button on her breeches. "Let's take all of this off. I am going to give you a bath."

6

LOS ANGELES, PRESENT DAY

Driving her new, black Tesla Model X down Venice Boulevard toward the movie studio, Saxon enjoyed the raspy voice of the latest country music star coming out of Nashville. The young singer filled every word with emotion as she sang about her cheating man. Saxon smiled, pleased to know the singer was doing so well. The rising star was the last Saxon had worked with before she disappeared from the country music scene altogether. Her instinct proved right once again as the song was destined for number one on the charts. Launching young singing careers was a lot of fun, and she missed the industry a little, but some things couldn't be helped. Instead, she was in Los Angeles about to sit in on a late evening read-through of the vampire hunter movie script. A reading centered on Faye Stapleton.

A tight feeling in Saxon's stomach started as she contemplated seeing the actress again. It had been a week, but not a moment passed that she didn't think of Faye. She knew so much about her from the research she did and even enjoyed sitting through Faye's biggest selling movies. Louis caught her in the act and, after making them popcorn with extra salt, sat down to watch too. At the end of one, he turned to her with his eyebrows raised. "This is your vampire hunter?" he asked. "America's sweetheart. She's so..." He paused and pursed his lips in thought.

"She's so...what?" Saxon asked, curious to hear what her closest confidant felt about the actress.

Louis shrugged. "Well," he said. "The word that comes to mind is cute." He held up a hand to stop Saxon from protesting. "Don't get me wrong, her charisma leaps off the screen. I can see why there's an attraction to her because she is a good actress. But I am struggling to see her as a ruthless hunter."

"I agree," Saxon said. "On the surface. But her audition... It was mesmerizing, and frankly, a little chilling."

They had left it at that, but Saxon did wonder as she turned into the entrance of the studio if, perhaps, she was wrong. The instant attraction and crackling chemistry between them may have swayed her judgment. Everyone was about to find out.

Rolling down her window, she stopped at the security booth at the entrance gate. The uniformed guard smiled and handed her a pass on a lanyard to show she was okay to be on the premises. "Good evening, Ms. Montague," he said. "New car?"

"Yes," she answered. "I was in the mood for black."

The man nodded. "Well, it's sweet. Always a Tesla though?" he asked, and Saxon nodded.

"Always," she replied. "I'm doing my part to save the planet. Needs to be around awhile."

The guard pushed the button to raise the gate. "Fair enough," he said with a grin, and Saxon drove through to go park in the lot closest to the building where they would hold the reading. As she was getting out of the car, she heard someone call her name. Turning to look, she saw one of the film producers coming her way from the parking lot. Dressed in khakis but with a button-down shirt and tie, the man was not as high up the ladder as the executive she spoke with poolside over a week before. Saxon knew he was working his way up the Hollywood ladder but still held a substantial interest in the movie's success.

"Hey," he said as Saxon slowed her pace. Headed the same direction, they fell into step. "Glad I caught you. About Faye Stapleton. Do you really—"

Saxon shook her head to silence him. She might have her doubts, but no one needed to know that. "She's the one we want for this," she said. "Give her a chance." The producer frowned and looked ready to argue further when Saxon gave him a look. "I insist." The man swallowed hard under her dark-eyed scrutiny, clearly seeing the authority on her face.

He held up his hands in surrender. "Okay," he said, as they walked through the outside door of the building. "Faye it is."

At the woman's name, Saxon's mouth went dry. She wasn't ready to see her yet, and spotting the women's restroom, Saxon turned toward the door to regroup. "I'll meet you in the conference room," she told him and ducked inside. Thankfully, the space was empty, so she didn't have to pretend to use it. Instead, she turned on the tap water to wash her hands. Looking at the mirror, she saw nothing but the three beige stall doors behind her. Used to the lack of a reflection, she didn't think anything of it until the restroom door opened. Saxon turned away from the mirror, knowing she needed to get out of the room, and then froze. Faye Stapleton had just walked in.

. . .

Head down, thinking of her lines from the script she would soon be reading from, Faye nearly ran into Saxon standing just inside the door. "Oh," was all she could think to say as the woman's eyes gazed into her own. Dark and mysterious eyes that made her heart do a flip-flop. Every bit of chemistry she felt during the audition came rushing back. Although she hadn't seen her for a week, Faye didn't seem able to stop thinking about the movie director. A half dozen debriefs with her best friend Jane about how unlikely a relationship would be did nothing to lessen the attraction. Unable to help herself, she'd googled Saxon Montague and read every article about her she could find. Considering the splash she made in Hollywood, there were shockingly few, and those were thin on details. No interviews and most puzzling, no photographs.

"Good evening," Saxon said, the slightest tremble in her words. Faye blinked. It almost seemed like the movie director felt affected by their sudden meeting too. She was sure she felt the air crackling between them.

Smiling, Faye recovered herself. "Good evening," she answered, working hard to keep her voice even. "Thank you again for this chance." For a beat, Saxon did not respond, and Faye was afraid she said the wrong thing. Maybe the director was having doubts about her choice in casting Faye as a vampire hunter masked as a gritty FBI profiler.

Thankfully, before Faye could have a complete panic attack at the idea, Saxon nodded. "I have a feeling about you," she murmured. Faye had to work to keep from shivering at the women's sexy-sounding comment and wanted to say something similar in return. She stepped a little closer, but before she could find the right words, Saxon suddenly stepped aside to let her pass. She was all business. "I'll see you in there." The change felt abrupt, and Faye wasn't sure what to think, but then Saxon was gone. Confused about what just happened, Faye looked in the mirror over the sinks and contemplated why Saxon would suddenly brush her off. There was a distinct possibility the woman felt the same chemistry but wanted to avoid a relationship. The very idea of dating the female director of the movie she was starring in was an epic disaster.

"What the hell am I going to do?" she said to her reflection, but her mirror image did not answer. She'd only come into the restroom to gather herself before walking into the conference room to read her part but found herself more flustered than ever. Having Saxon in the same room with her all evening would be a challenge. There was no denying the woman's mere presence sent Faye's heart racing. "Get a grip. I'm not a rookie."

She knew what she needed to do and that was pretend Saxon wasn't there. Just like how the movie director stormed out of the bathroom to avoid any more awkwardness between them, Faye would do the same. Saxon Montague was nothing but an ordinary person directing a movie. She'd dealt with over a dozen others just like her. Except for the raging chemistry between them, but she was choosing not to think about that. Taking a deep breath, Faye squared her shoulders. She would walk out the door and straight into the conference room to give the performance of her life. It was showtime.

Saxon hated rushing out of the restroom, but she couldn't risk Faye looking past her and into the mirror. She was rude, and she knew it. The confused expression on the woman's face was the last thing Saxon wanted to see. Still, the electricity between them, an almost physical pull, was dangerous as well. Becoming involved with Faye was a mistake on every possible level. Professionally, of course, but that was not the only reason. Crossing the hallway toward the door leading to the conference room, she considered the second reason. Saxon was simply too attracted to her. Even though Louis told her to follow her heart, there would be nothing but pain in the end.

As she approached the entrance, a flicker of movement to her left caught her eye. She would normally have registered the footsteps if she weren't so distracted. Looking, Saxon saw a short, young woman with straight black hair down past her shoulders rushing up to her. "Ms. Montague," she said, slightly out of breath. "I'm so glad I caught up with you."

Unsure who the stranger was, Saxon furrowed her brow. "Have we met?" she asked, just as she noticed the temporary press pass around the woman's neck. Talking to a reporter was the last thing she wanted, and she kept walking, eager to get inside and away from any questions.

"No," the reporter said, ignoring the unhappy expression on Saxon's face. "But if you don't mind, I have a few questions about the movie. Is it true you were the one who insisted Faye Stapleton play the lead?"

"Yes," Saxon said, unwilling to go into any detail. She reached for the door handle, ready to get away. Amazingly, the young woman had the nerve to slip between her and the door until they were standing nose to nose. Saxon had to stop or plow into her. A part of her was starting to get angry, but she clamped the feeling down. Anger was a dangerous emotion, and the last thing she wanted was to show anything suspicious to a reporter.

"Just a few more questions," the reporter said, relentless and showing no fear of reprisal. She was a reporter hungry for a story. Getting the reclusive movie director to talk would be a huge career booster.

Saxon didn't care. "Please move," she hissed, but the reporter was relentless.

"Why Faye Stapleton? She has no experience in a film like this and frankly seems like a horrible choice."

"Oh really?" Saxon heard from not too far behind her. She knew the voice. Faye had overheard the conversation and was walking to join them. "And who are you exactly?"

The reporter's eyes were wide with excitement. Clearly, the circumstances could not be better for her. Not only had she cornered Saxon Montague, but she would be able to interview America's sweetheart too. Wasting no time, the reporter launched into a barrage of questions. "Why do you think you can pull this off? Have you two met before now? What if the movie is a flop?"

A growl of frustration started to rise in Saxon's throat, but Faye saved her. Clearly used to overzealous reporters, she gave the woman a formidable look. "Move out of the way," she said in a calm but firm voice. "Or I'm calling security. You shouldn't even be in this building." She tilted her head. "Let me guess, you got a press pass to cover the advanced movie screening on the other side of the lot and snuck away."

The reporter grinned. "You can't blame a girl for trying," she said but did move out from in front of the door. "But at least let me take a picture of you two together." Saxon noticed for the first time the woman was holding her cellphone down by her side. She wondered if the whole conversation was being recorded or if she had tried taking a picture from down the hall before she ran up. Not that it mattered because nothing would be in the shot, and like everyone else, the reporter would blame it on the phone. A photo up close with Faye would be a disaster.

"No," Saxon said, harsher than she intended. Checking her emotions again, she made her face relax. The last thing she wanted was to pique the woman's curiosity if she overreacted. "We're late as it is."

"She's right," Faye agreed, pushing past Saxon to open the door. "And I better never see you hanging out around here again." Without another word, she went inside with Saxon following in her wake.

7

LOS ANGELES, PRESENT DAY

The conference room had grown hot and stuffy. Over a dozen actors sat around the folding tables set up in a horseshoe pattern. People who were a part of the film for other reasons sat in chairs along the wall. They were well into their third hour of reading, having started and stopped at parts, and the hour grew late. Finally, Faye flipped to the last page of the script. "The end," the second assistant director said, having been the one to read all the none speaking parts to maintain the flow of the reading. The room let out a collective breath of relief. Faye included. Although she felt things had gone well enough with her part, she was also aware that one of the movie's producers was watching her closely. The situation wasn't helped by Saxon sitting somewhere behind her. However, she decided that it was better than being able to see her the whole time. Being distracted by their chemistry would have thrown her off altogether.

Speaking of which, the movie director walked to the front of the room to stand with the producer. Clearly more composed than in the restroom, she looked confident and sexy, and Faye couldn't stop herself from biting her lip. "That was well done," the producer said with a grin, and Faye tried to refocus. "I'm feeling better about this movie every second." He turned to Saxon. "I think we might have another blockbuster on our hands."

Faye watched Saxon nod but barely smile, humble in her response. "I agree," was all she said. Not for the first time, Faye was struck by how mature the woman seemed considering she looked like she was barely able to drink. She worked on a couple films where the actors were in their twenties and overly confident, almost arrogant, and a little wild off set. There was no evidence Saxon acted that way, and it was just another mysterious thing about her personality.

The producer paused, apparently waiting for Saxon to say more, but when she didn't, he shrugged. "Well okay," he said with a nervous laugh. "That's it for now. See you all next week."

At his cue, people gathered their things and stood to leave. One of the costars, the woman who would play the LAPD detective, stopped beside Faye.

"Hey," she said, smiling. "That was great. Really."

Faye tried not to hear the hint of surprise in her voice and smiled back. "Thank you," she said. "Same to you." While she stood there, a few other actors in the movie breezed by, saying things like 'Good job' and 'Can't wait to work with you.' The positive feedback felt terrific, and she thanked them all.

"No bullshit," a man's voice said. "You rocked that." Faye looked to see tall, blond, and ridiculously handsome Brad Norris standing beside her. He was the leading man in the movie and played the vampire serial killer she would be hunting. The actor was a big name and no doubt making five times as much money as she was to do the film, but that was nothing new. He had a legendary ego and was also infamous for dating, not to mention sleeping with his female costars so he could make the cover of the tabloids. So far, they hadn't worked together, because he would never dare lower himself to rom-com material.

Still, Faye wanted to start off on the right foot, so she gave him her biggest smile. "Thank you, Brad. That means a lot coming from you," she said and watched him glow under the praise. His eyes roamed her face, and she worried maybe she laid it on a little thick. The last thing Faye wanted was to give him the wrong idea.

"Are you leaving?" he said, and before she could answer yes or no, he leaned closer. "It's dark out there, so let me walk you to your car." His offer was not what she wanted, hoping to say something more to Saxon, but when she looked over at the movie director the woman averted her eyes. There was no doubt she had been watching Faye and Brad but continued to look away. Her body language made it clear she didn't want to interact.

Frustrated, but not letting it show else she make a fool of herself, Faye looked at Brad. "Okay," she said. "That is nice of you."

As Faye and Brad Norris left the conference room together, Saxon wondered for the first time if she misread the actress and her preferences. There was always the possibility she had no attraction to women. Still, Saxon narrowed her eyes and thought back to how they looked at each other in the restroom earlier. The smoldering passion beating just below the surface. She felt the attraction was mutual without a doubt, but perhaps Faye didn't recognize the feelings for what they were. In her research of Faye Stapleton leading up to today, Saxon read of the few liaisons the actress had over her career. They all seemed to run the same course. Hot at the beginning with lots of photos and headlines of them having dinner or going on vacations at the beach. Then, things would quietly fall apart, again making headlines. Regardless, they were short, and in Saxon's opinion, appeared meaningless. It seemed more likely to Saxon that Faye Stapleton was a lesbian but needed to keep it a secret. Few people in Hollywood could sustain coming out of the closet.

"I think you may be right," the producer said, interrupting her thoughts. "Faye did a good job reading the part today."

Saxon nodded. "Yes, she did."

"But can she pull it off on screen?" he added. "That will be the question."

He was right, but for some reason Saxon felt entirely confident Faye would be successful. The edginess was there, although a bit buried. As the director, Saxon needed to coax that part out, and because of the connection she felt between them, she believed that she could. In fact, there was no reason not to start discussing the role with her already, and she wondered if the actress had left the lot yet. "If you'll excuse me," she said to the producer who she realized was still talking to her, though she hadn't heard a word. Something about wanting to find the perfect eerie coffin for the vampire in the movie to sleep in. It took all of Saxon's considerable restraint to keep from rolling her eyes. The use of coffins myth was just another misconception. One of many she knew would be a part of *Venandi* and a reason, among others, why she hadn't wanted to do this film.

"What do you think?" the producer asked, and Saxon

tried to pick up on the thread of the conversation. If the man wanted a coffin in the movie, she would give it to him. It wasn't like she could argue the validity of vampires sleeping all day by telling him they actually never slept. She could tell him they binge-watch a lot of Netflix but decided against it. Somethings, Saxon couldn't share.

Giving the answer her best guess, she shrugged. "Why not have it be a sarcophagus?" she suggested, and the producer raised his eyebrows.

"I think you are confusing your horror plots," he said, sounding shocked at the idea. "Mummies come out of a sarcophagus."

Saxon smiled, finding the entire conversation humorous. The man looked so serious about his answer. "You're right," she said. "Coffin it is then. Now, I have an appointment, so I will see you in a week." Not bothering to wait for an answer, she strode from the conference room, intent on finding Faye if she was still on the premises.

Faye stayed silent while Brad went on about his latest vacation to the French Riviera with a pretty, young actress she knew of but had never met. If she had to guess, Faye would say there were at least twenty years between their ages. Not that it mattered necessarily, but she did wonder if perhaps Brad Norris was headed for a midlife crisis. The thought of age gaps brought her around to Saxon once again. Everything seemed to do that, and she was beginning to wonder why she tried to fight it. Still, the movie director had to be over ten if not more years younger, and that fact was only another reason she needed to walk away from whatever was growing between them.

Reaching her car, Faye refocused on Brad. "This is me,"

she said, motioning to the white convertible BMW. "I guess I'll see you in a week."

Brad leaned on the side of the car, striking a pose Faye wondered if other women found sexy. He looked relaxed, yet she was sure he was flexing his pecs under his polo shirt. Men were so not her thing. "Hey, what's the hurry?" he said. "I thought maybe we could discuss getting together to practice. Maybe start with dinner tonight."

Faye was not even sure what 'start with dinner' meant, but she was not interested. "Actually, I'm tired, and the rest of the week, I'm booked up with interviews about getting this role," she said. "But I appreciate the offer."

Brad frowned, clearly not used to being so flatly refused. "You can't be busy every second," he said, leaning toward her a little and gazing his blue eyes into her own hazel ones. Again, Faye was struck with the idea the well-practiced look he was giving her melted most women until they were wet between their legs. All she did was smile.

"I'm afraid I am," she said, and a look of irritation crossed the actor's handsome face. Faye suddenly knew she needed to be careful. Making him feel insulted could make shooting the movie difficult. "But really, I am so flattered."

Narrowing his eyes, Brad looked ready to say something more, when suddenly someone else cleared their throat. Both Faye and Brad started at the sudden interruption, and when they looked, Saxon stood at the end of the BMW. "Faye, I was hoping to have a word with you," she said, and Faye let out a sigh of relief. It was clear that Brad Norris was not going to simply take no for an answer, and she didn't know how she would handle the situation. Thankfully, she didn't have to with Saxon's arrival.

"Hey," Brad said, standing straighter in Saxon's presence. "Real honor to work with you. Your stuff is moody and cool." He glanced at Faye. "We can talk more about dinner later, but I'm pretty busy." Then, without a look back, he left the two of them standing by the car.

They both watched him strut away before Saxon looked at her. "Is everything okay?" she asked, clearly having picked up on the tension she walked up on.

"It's fine," Faye answered. "Nothing I can't handle." She looked into Saxon's eyes. "But thank you for coming over. What did you want to talk to me about?"

Saxon was quiet for a moment, and her eyes searched Faye's face before stopping at her mouth. Her look was so sensual and undeniably full of heat, she felt a throb rise from her center. Unlike Brad, Saxon definitely had an effect on her. Drawn by a force she couldn't resist, Faye slid closer. Saxon's eyes snapped back to her own, and the lust there flashed to a hint of warning, but it did not keep Faye from leaning in. Their faces were close and although Faye knew kissing the movie director here in front of the world was the worst idea imaginable, she wanted to anyway. The moment held, and neither of them moved. "Thank you for helping me with the reporter earlier," Saxon said quietly, but Faye felt the thrum of intensity behind the words. The movie director wanted her. The idea of such intensity in such a short amount of time surprised her, but there was no mistaking chemistry. And with Saxon, the feeling was off the charts.

She licked her lips. "You're welcome," she said. "They can be so pushy." Saxon nodded, their eyes still holding. They were going to kiss, and Faye was thankful for the darkened parking lot. Before they moved, she heard someone calling her name. Jerking back, as if she had been in a trance, she looked around. A studio security guard was coming their way.

Stepping back, a little flustered, Faye plastered a smile on her face. "Hi," she said to the guard. "Is everything okay?"

The guard stopped in front of her and held out an envelope. "I'm glad I caught up to you," he said. "I noticed this under your windshield wiper earlier and was afraid the thing might blow away, so I held onto it for you."

Faye stared at the offering and knew the letter inside was from her stalker. Somehow, he or she had gained access to the studio lot and knew her car. With a shaking hand, she took it from the guard. "Thank you," she murmured, stuffing the thing in her leather shoulder bag, but not before she registered her name scrawled on the front with a little black heart.

Obviously not noticing her discomfort, the guard gave a little salute and started away. "Have a good night," he said and then was gone back the way he came. Without having to look, she knew Saxon's eyes were on her, but she didn't want to explain her situation. The last thing Faye wanted was to be a problem and cause the movie director to doubt she should be in the film. No one needed extra hassles in an already complex process.

Growing more upset by the moment, she wanted to leave. "I need to go," she said and unlocked her car door without meeting Saxon's eyes. "See you in a week." Before waiting for an answer, she got in and started the car. The last thing she saw as she drove away was the woman looking at her, and she couldn't shake the thought Saxon somehow knew what was going on. And she didn't look happy about it.

8

LOS ANGELES, PRESENT DAY

The week was one of the longest of Saxon's life, which was saying a lot. Time and again, she thought of contacting Faye on some excuse about details on the movie. She even went so far as thinking of inviting her to dinner, but then would end up angry at herself for wanting something she should not. Sticking to her boundaries was all she could do. Barely. Thankfully, the waiting was finally over as the filming would begin that night. As twilight fell, she walked the location with her first assistant director and cinematographer. Everyone agreed the look and feel of the selected spot were perfect. They were shooting an intense night scene, and Saxon was determined to start the movie off right. "I want a dolly shot," Saxon explained, pointing from the curb to the back of the warehouse. "When Faye gets out of her car and walks to the victim found behind the dumpster."

"Got it," the first assistant director said. "I'll get the guys moving." He was already keying his microphone to give the order as Saxon turned to the cinematographer. She had worked with him on the last film and respected his talent.

"Low-key lighting sound good to you?" she asked, sincerely wanting his opinion. "Lots of contrast with some shadow."

The cinematographer grinned. "Yeah," he said, excitement in his eyes. "That would work well. A classic approach that sets a dark mood."

"Exactly," Saxon said, walking away to let her team do their work. Being notified ten minutes ago that Faye was on set, she hoped to catch her before she went into hair and makeup. Forcing herself to contain her excitement over seeing the actress again, she rounded the corner of Faye's private trailer. Just as she was about to knock on the door, she realized the actress was talking to someone on speakerphone. She was able to hear every word and, disappointed, started to back away. Then, she heard Faye say her name and paused.

"Saxon was crazy to pick me," Faye said, panic in her tone. "I do rom-coms for God's sake. What was she thinking? And now, when I mess this up, the producers, hell, everyone in the industry, are going to tell her I told you so."

"Faye, stop," said a woman's voice on the other end of the call. "We've practiced, and you know every line."

"It's not that," Faye said. "What if I'm not convincing? I mean, a vampire hunter. Really?"

Saxon heard enough. She couldn't let Faye psych herself out anymore and knocked on the trailer's door. "I need to go," Faye said, clearly still talking to the other person. "I think I'm being called to hair and makeup."

"Call me as soon as you've finished the scene," the other woman said.

"I will," Saxon heard Faye say and then the trailer door opened. The actress stood in the doorway, looking completely caught off guard to see Saxon. "Oh... it's you."

Saxon smiled. "Yes, me," she said. "May I come in?"

Faye nodded and, without a word, backed up to let her climb the three metal steps to enter. When they were face to face, Saxon did her best to stay entirely professional. This was not the time to let her attraction get in the way. Still, seeing Faye after a week of thinking of nothing but her did make it hard to concentrate. A look into the actress' eyes and Saxon knew she felt something too. Swallowing hard, Saxon pressed on. "I wanted to talk to you about tonight's scene for a few minutes."

"Tonight's scene," Faye repeated, looking distracted to the point she wasn't even registering what Saxon said. She licked her lips, and Saxon could not stop staring at her mouth. For weeks, the thought of kissing Faye haunted her, and at this moment, she could not resist, professional or not. Stepping forward while the woman did the same, their mouths collided in a fiery kiss. Everything she imagined about how kissing Faye would feel did not compare to the surge of desire that filled Saxon. Sliding her arms around Faye's waist, she pulled her in tight, making the actress gasp with excitement. Wanting her, all of her, Saxon ran her hands up under the back of the woman's blouse. Her skin was deliciously hot to the touch. What they were doing was crazy, and there was no time for that, yet she didn't care. She wanted Faye. Needed her.

Suddenly, there was a knock at the door of the trailer, and they both froze. "They're ready for you in makeup," came the sound of a production assistant's voice. Saxon stifled a growl of frustration while the two of them broke apart. Faye's breath came fast, and Saxon's hunger to kiss her more made her ache. The knock came again. "Ms. Stapleton?"

"I'll be right out," Faye finally managed, and Saxon knew their opportunity had passed, but hopefully not forever.

Faye sat in the fake police squad car and waited to start her scene. Her lips still burned with the feel of Saxon's mouth on hers, and she had trouble believing they kissed not more than an hour before in her trailer. Everything about it was wrong, and yet, felt so right. When the woman pulled her in tighter, and they were body to body, Faye felt passion like she never had before. Saxon's magnetism was powerful, and if not for the knock on the door, she wasn't sure where things would have ended.

"Ms. Stapleton," the second assistant director said through the car's open window, interrupting Faye's erotic thoughts. "We'll be ready to start in three minutes."

"Thank you," she said, although the news made Faye's stomach tighten with anxiety. She needed to get her head back in the game and forget about Saxon and kisses and what it all meant. Right now, she needed to be an FBI profiler at the scene of the crime. Getting out of the car, Faye took in her surroundings. The red and blue splash of police emergency lights against the dark almost black-looking brick of the warehouse set a somber tone. The action was for her to walk up to the rusted and dirty green dumpster to meet with the two uniformed LAPD police officers who made the discovery. A plainclothes detective was also in the scene, and they would discuss the grisly events and the nearly decapitated body. A production assistant had already brought her polaroid shots of the 'mutilated' actor so she wouldn't be caught off guard by how disgusting things looked and overreact. Considering how well the special effects makeup artist had done, Faye appreciated knowing ahead of time. One of the police officers was supposed to be puking right after the scene started, and Faye did not want to join him in real life.

Saxon walked out of the shadows but did not look in Faye's direction and she was thankful the director was showing discretion. One look into those sultry dark eyes would ruin Faye for the shot. The last thing she would be able to think about was slaying a vampire. While she watched, Saxon gave the camera crew final instructions and then faded back into the shadows. The second assistant camera operator stepped forward with the clapperboard in hand and looked to Faye. "Are you ready, Ms. Stapleton?" he asked, and she let out a long, slow breath.

"Yes," she answered, and the man called out the scene number and take one before clapping the filmsticks loudly together. There was a pause as the cameras began rolling, and then Faye heard Saxon's voice.

"Action."

In that instant, Faye blocked out everything but the scene she was performing. Dressed in a charcoal gray trench coat over black slacks and an off-white blouse, she began her walk. The sound of the low-heeled dress boots she wore tapped faintly on the asphalt. No obvious makeup, and her hair flowed in blonde waves past her shoulders. In an understated way, there was no denying she looked beautiful, but for her eyes. Those looked ruthless. Cold and purposeful. The cameras caught every bit of the gravity coming off her. This was a woman on a mission.

Faye heard the policeman puking and saw the dead woman's pale, bare legs behind the dumpster. She watched as the LAPD detective turned to her and raised an eyebrow. "Can I help you?" the detective asked with a frown.

Without missing a step, Faye flipped open her FBI identification and held up the wallet for her. "Agent Kolchak," she replied. "Profiler." She didn't bother to say anything else as she slipped under the yellow police tape to survey the scene under the spotlights.

"Hey, what the hell...?" the second police officer said, but the LAPD detective waved him off. Faye was putting off a don't mess with me aura, and so everyone stayed silent while she looked the corpse over. It was not a pretty sight. The girl's eyes were open wide with fear, and her throat was ripped out, down to the white bone of the spinal column. Blood from the jugular should have splashed everywhere, but it hadn't. Faye narrowed her eyes. A look of certainty set on her face as if she'd seen this before. As if she knew without a doubt what had happened.

Saxon watched Faye standing at the body's feet studying it. A chill had run through her as the scene played out. The lighting was spot on, and watching the dolly shot on the camera monitor told her they framed it perfectly. Faye had a confident, almost arrogant, way about her that was ideal for her character. Yet when she looked at the body, a hint of sympathy showed in her eyes one moment but then went hard, angry. The actress played the part to precision. "Cut," Saxon said at the end of the scene.

"Damn," said the script supervisor sitting in a folding chair beside her. "Did she nail that? I mean, she did, right?"

Saxon nodded. "She did," she murmured, and when Faye finally turned to face her, she knew the actress was aware of it too. She smiled, and it lit up her face, which just a minute before was that of a coldhearted vampire hunter.

"Do we reset, Saxon?" the cameraman asked.

Saxon, pleased to be able to shake her head said, "No."

She noted the surprise on the man's face. It was rare to only go with one take, but her instincts told her this one was perfect. Any others would lose the edge of being new. "Break this down and set up for the tighter angles in the next scene." She slipped from her director's chair excited to see Faye walking toward her. As the woman neared, Saxon felt desire building inside her. During the scene, she forced herself to ignore the feel of their kiss and the ache it left behind. With the shot over, all the cravings rushed back, but so did a fear she had gone too far.

"We aren't doing it again?" Faye asked, her eyebrows raised. "Really?"

Saxon nodded, locking eyes with the actress. "Really. Close-ups are next, but we have a few minutes." Glancing around to make sure no one was standing nearby, she cleared her throat, knowing she needed to apologize for earlier. She leaned in to keep her voice down. "Faye, I'm sorry about what happened in the trailer. It was—"

"No," Faye said, soft but adamant. "I'm not sorry." Saxon sucked in a breath, feeling the passion behind the woman's answer. They were thinking the same thing and the desire she felt bloomed even hotter.

"Have dinner with me tomorrow after shooting," she blurted and then recovered her composure. "To talk about next week's scenes with Brad. The interactions with the vampire will be critical."

Faye's eyes became even brighter. "Yes," she said, her voice breathless. "I want that too."

9

LOS ANGELES, PRESENT DAY

"Tell me everything," Jane said, taking off her sunglasses as she slipped onto the stool at the island in Faye's kitchen. "I mean everything."

Smiling, Faye, still in her workout clothes from her morning yoga, brought over two big ceramic mugs of coffee she had just made with her French Press. She loved the deep, rich flavor the method captured, not to mention the process relaxed her. Cooking was one of her passions, but she hardly found any time at all during the making of a movie. The previous evening, they wrapped filming well past midnight. It was only eight a.m., but that was the only opportunity she had an extra hour to talk to Jane. She'd tried a phone call, but Jane would have none of it. After dropping her two boys off at school, she had come straight over. Faye was glad she had insisted because she really needed to talk to her best friend. Biting her lip, she tried to think of where to begin. There was a lot to talk about.

"She asked me to dinner," Faye finally said. "For after filming tonight."

Jane's jaw dropped, and she blinked at Faye. "Saxon

Montague asked you out?" she said slowly. "Oh, my God. Faye, I hope you said yes."

"Of course, I did," Faye said with a grin and then lowered her eyes to play with her coffee mug. "But there's more..."

Jane, about to sip her coffee, set it back down untouched. "More?"

Faye felt a blush rising up on her neck. "We kissed," she said, and when Jane covered her mouth with her hand before letting out a squeal of excitement, she laughed. "And it was amazing. Like, took my breath away."

"Where? When? Details!" Jane asked, then leaned closer as if they were discussing a conspiracy. "Is that all you did?"

Faye nodded. "We kissed in my trailer right before I went to hair and makeup," she replied. "When we were on speakerphone, it was Saxon who knocked." Then, she leaned in too, matching Jane's excitement. Last night really was incredible and thinking of the kiss made her stomach flutter with anticipation of what might be waiting ahead. "And that's all we did because a PA knocked and interrupted us. But I swear, I'd have ripped her clothes off if we were anywhere else."

"Wow," Jane said, waving a hand to cool off her neck. "I can't believe it. Not that you want to rip her clothes off, I mean, but that you're possibly going to have a chance to."

"I know," Faye whispered. The reality that later that night, she would be alone with Saxon Montague made her heart race. The day's filming was going to be long and anticipation would make it extremely hard to stay in character. Luckily, all the shots were indoors with lots of dialogue and less set up, so they should finish much earlier than the previous night. And then—dinner with Saxon.

Jane grabbed her forearm. "What will you wear?" she

asked, suddenly all business. "You need to knock her socks off. But not be super obvious."

Faye shrugged. "I'll probably wear whatever I am in when I arrive on set," she answered, assuming they would go to dinner immediately after they stopped for the day. "I can't exactly show up in a little black cocktail dress. As attracted as I am to her, I'm not ready to come out to Hollywood yet."

"You're right," Jane said, and then her eyes widened. "Is she out?"

Faye shook her head. "I don't think so from what I read, but then there's almost nothing on her. Especially when it comes to her personal life."

Jane picked up her coffee. "Well, at least you confirmed one thing," she said, then took a sip while eyeing Faye over the rim.

"And what's that?" Faye asked her closest friend.

Grinning, Jane took a sip before answering. "That she's into women," she said, and Faye grinned too. She most definitely had.

After twenty-three takes of the last scene of the day, Saxon was about to pull her short hair out. Ironically, the shot was the same part of the script Faye performed for her audition. A reasonably straightforward exchange between the FBI profiler and the pathologist discussing the cause of death of the young woman found behind the dumpster. The problem was not Faye. She stayed in character and delivered her lines perfectly. However, the man playing the pathologist could not seem to get through the dialogue correctly or convincingly. The irony wasn't lost on Saxon that this was happening when all she wanted to do was call it for the day and go spend every minute she could with Faye.

To make the situation worse, she couldn't say anything about why she wanted the day to be over. Naturally, the whole crew was ready to go home. Still, nothing compared to how excited Saxon was at the thought of being near Faye later. Alone. By the way Faye was avoiding all eye contact, she imagined the actress felt the same. At least they were in an unspoken agreement that their plans should be a secret. Only during the few moments when Saxon gave her specific directions for a scene did they even speak to each other. Those moments were thick with chemistry. It was all she could do not to run a finger over the back of Faye's hand or take in the scent of her hair. Finally, though, the day wound down. "Meet me in the parking lot?" Saxon whispered to Faye as she walked by her on the way off the set.

All Faye did was give a brief nod and keep going. A look around, and Saxon confirmed there was no evidence anyone noticed or was listening. They needed to keep things that way, more for Faye's reputation than Saxon's. No one had been able to confirm Saxon's sexual leanings as she'd never done an interview nor dated anyone since she splashed onto the Hollywood scene. If it came out she was gay, people might make a big deal of it, but her career would survive. Considering how mysterious everyone said she was, the news would probably boost her career.

It would not be the same for Faye, which made her question if this was the right thing to be doing. The actress had so much to lose over an affair, and Saxon knew their chance at anything long term was impossible. At some point, Saxon would have to disappear in the middle of the night. It was one reason she didn't let herself get attached to anyone anymore. For Saxon, her heart would always belong to another. Yet, with Faye, she felt something different than in the past. Something fresh and exciting, and she wanted to explore it even if only for a short time.

A knock on the passenger window brought her out of her thoughts, and she rolled it down. Faye leaned in. The sight of her face alone made Saxon a little weak. Maybe what they were doing would end badly, but right at this moment, she did not care. She wanted this woman, and there had been far too many long and lonely years when Saxon cared about no one at all. "Hi," Faye said, a blush on her cheeks. Excitement, with a hint of nervousness, shone in her eyes. "Can you give a girl a lift?"

Saxon smiled and leaned across the console to pull the door handle before pushing it open. "Nothing I want more," she murmured, and it was true. Tonight, she only wanted Faye.

They drove toward Santa Monica from downtown Los Angeles planning to go to a hole in the wall diner Faye sometimes visited. It was a place where tourists didn't frequent. Luckily, it was well past eight, and the evening traffic was light, although the sexual tension in the car was not. Faye licked her lips and wished she dared to tell Saxon to skip the restaurant and instead they could do takeout from her place. The magnitude of desire she felt for the movie director was off the charts. Her charisma and their chemistry were phenomenal. In her opinion, Saxon Montague should be the actress in the movie because she had no doubt people would flock to see her on the screen. Fans would line up down the block to look into those dark, mysterious, all-consuming eyes. Eyes that seemed to see all of her and made her body throb.

"You were great today," Saxon said, catching her in the middle of sexy thoughts. Faye blushed a little but hoped the dark car made her reaction less obvious. "I'm sorry that the last scene took so many takes."

Faye shrugged, thankful for a topic to discuss rather than sit in her seat squirming as she lusted over Saxon. "I've been through worse," she said. "You were the one who was the most patient." She laughed. "And when the corpse sneezed..."

Saxon chuckled. "That did bring down the house for a few minutes," she agreed. "I'll save it for the after-credits blooper reel."

Faye studied Saxon's profile in the shadows cast by car headlights passing. The woman was so attractive with her strong features softened by full lips. Such kissable lips. Faye swallowed to contain herself. "You're really good at this," she said, trying to think of something to say. "Film making, I mean. Where did you learn so much without anyone ever hearing of you?"

Saxon was quiet, and Faye worried she'd said the wrong thing. The director was obviously very private about her life, but before she could apologize, Saxon glanced at her. "Thank you," she said. "That means a lot coming from someone who's as experienced as you are. I've watched your films."

"Oh God," Faye said, pressing back into the passenger seat. "Not all of them I hope," she said. "I'm not too proud of some of the earlier ones. I was just eye candy."

Saxon chuckled. "You are America's sweetheart," she said, and Faye playfully slapped her on the shoulder but then let her hand linger. The black, synthetic leather jacket she was wearing was cool under Faye's fingertips, and unable to help herself, she ran them up to touch the woman's exposed neck. When Saxon let out the tiniest of moans at the contact, she knew going to the restaurant would be nothing but torture for them both. The question was, what to do about it? She knew this was the time to be bold or not at all.

"I'm incredibly attracted to you," Faye whispered, hoping she wasn't making a complete fool of herself. "Being in this car so close is driving me wild."

Turning her head just enough, Saxon kissed the tips of Faye's fingers. The touch, although cool, seemed to burn against her skin, and Faye gasped. The contact was almost too much to bear. "I feel the same," she said and then paused, clearly conflicted as to what to do next. They were crazy to do anything but go to dinner and get to know each other, but Faye had never been so turned on so easily.

"Take me home with you," Faye whispered, and Saxon answered by putting on her turn signal to take them off the freeway. The next exit was for the Pacific Coast Highway and not the way to downtown Santa Monica and the restaurant. They headed straight for Malibu.

10

S team rose all around her as Saxon tentatively stepped a foot into the hot bathwater. All her years growing up, there was never anything like this. When they had bathed on the tobacco farm, it was with a basin of water from the pump out back. The only time she ever took a full-body bath was in the creek at the height of summer. Washing in warmed water in a white, porcelain, clawfoot bathtub was beyond her imagination. But then, so much had been over the last few hours. Everything about Susan was surreal, and Saxon wished the night would never end.

Feeling the warmth of the water envelop her as she sat, Saxon let out a sigh. She wasn't sure if everything she felt came from drinking the absinthe or just the result of sensory overload. Either way, she didn't care. This was bliss. A half dozen candles flickered from the shelf on the wall above her. They gave off the sweet scent of lavender and cast a sensual light around the room. Once Saxon settled, Susan lowered herself to a short stool to sit beside the tub, close enough to touch. Only then did Saxon realize the beautiful woman was not getting undressed to join her. Not that she thought Susan was unclean, but Saxon, if she was honest with herself, wanted to see her naked.

"You're not coming in the water with me?" she asked, and Susan smiled.

"No," she said. "I want to wash you instead." Then she paused. "Is that all right with you?"

Saxon nodded, feeling suddenly a little self-conscious at being the only one naked, but also incredibly aroused at the idea of Susan's hands on her body. "Yes," she finally said. "I would like that."

"Good," Susan answered with a small smile. "May I unbraid your hair?"

"Yes," Saxon said. No one had unbraided her hair but herself since her mother died. The thought of a beautiful woman doing it tonight was both touching and erotic.

Susan reached for Saxon's hair and pulled the rawhide tie free. "Thank you," she said as her fingers slipped the braid apart and let the hair fall over Saxon's back and shoulders. The tickle from the contact made Saxon shiver with excitement. With a hum of pleasure, Susan picked up a ceramic pitcher from a tray beside her before trickling the warm water on Saxon's head and over her long, brown hair. "Does that feel good?"

There were no words to describe how good the sensation felt, and when Susan ran her fingers through the damp locks, Saxon thought she might die. Nothing in her twenty-one years had ever felt so good. But that was just the beginning. Setting the pitcher aside, Susan picked up a small cake of French milled soap from the metal tray hanging over the side of the tub. Again, there was the smell of lavender as the woman wet the soap in the bathwater. "I'm going to wash your hair first," Susan said as she lathered the soap. "Let me know if this feels okay."

With that, she rubbed the soap into Saxon's hair, working the stands to make them clean and soft. The contact was so intense, so electrified, that Saxon felt it radiate through every part of her body. Most especially between her legs. Susan began to wash her with both hands, piling the hair up on top of her head, until it was cleaner than perhaps it had ever been. "That feels incredible," Saxon gasped as Susan rinsed her with a second pitcher on the tray. "You have no idea."

"Oh, I think I might," Susan said, picking up a soft, white, cotton washcloth from the tray. Wetting it, she rubbed soap into the cloth before making slow circles on Saxon's back until it was coated with suds. "Lean back," Susan whispered and Saxon did, resting against the cool ceramic. "I want to wash your front too."

Unable to control it, a moan of anticipation came from Saxon's throat. Susan started slowly, sliding the soapy cloth along Saxon's neck. Then, lower onto her chest, just above her full breasts. Saxon felt her nipples, already hard from the idea of things ahead, tighten to an ache. Clearly seeing the pink tips darken, Susan hummed again, pleasure radiating from her. "You like this?" she asked into Saxon's ear. The pulse inside Saxon grew stronger—more intense—to the point she knew there would have to be a release soon or she might go mad. Susan did not make her wait and instead moved the soapy swirling across one breast, coating the nipple with suds. Saxon sucked in a breath when Susan gave the hard tip a little squeeze.

"Yes," Saxon gasped in answer to her question. "I like this so much." Unable to sit still, she shifted in the tub, hoping to lessen the throb between her legs.

Susan chuckled knowingly and moved her hand with the washcloth over to the other breast. Again, she circled the nipple for a moment and then gave it a pinch. Out of reflex, Saxon reached for Susan's hand as if to guide it lower, but the woman pulled back. "Patience, darling," she said. "Let me do this my way. I promise, we are only just beginning." Saxon put her arm back on the side of the tub and tried to stay relaxed. Her desire to please Susan was as strong as her own needs, so she would obey for the moment.

Returning to her task, Susan rinsed the washcloth and set it aside so she could cup handfuls of water to dribble across Saxon's soapy breasts. As she rinsed them, the woman let her fingertips trail across Saxon's sensitive skin with each scoop. After washing away the soap, Susan slipped her fingers lower across Saxon's tight stomach. Her body was fit and hard from working the farm from dawn until dusk. "Oh God," Saxon moaned when the woman grazed the top of the dark, curly hair between her legs. She started to pant with anticipation, her entire body shaking she was so ready.

"Do you ever touch yourself?" Susan asked, and Saxon knew what she meant.

She bit her lip. "I live with my father and two brothers," she said. "And there isn't much privacy."

Susan nodded, sliding her fingers back and forth over the hair, teasing, almost taunting. "But you want to?" she asked, her own tone sounding more excited.

Saxon swallowed hard. There was no reason to hide the truth, even if Susan was a stranger. "All the time," she answered. "Especially after we go to town and I see the shopkeeper's daughter."

"Oh, really?" Susan murmured. "What does she look like?"

Smiling, Saxon sighed. "Beautiful. Long blonde hair always pulled up with a whalebone pin her grandmother sent from France," she said. "She never wears anything but different blue gingham dresses her mother makes her. They all match her eyes. So big and blue I feel like I'm falling into them when she looks at me."

Susan slipped her fingers a little lower in response. "Do you now," she said, and it wasn't a question but sounded like an observation. "And if she were to touch you like this? Would you like it?" Then, with a practiced hand, she slid one finger down and spread Saxon's lips, grazing her clit, and making Saxon shout out.

"Yes," she cried, her hips bucking in response.

"And why is that?" Susan asked, pulling her finger back to tickle her clit again.

Saxon licked her lips, breathing heavily. "Because I want her," she admitted. "Ever since we were in school together." Susan responded by circling Saxon's center in slow, methodical movements making the woman moan. Gripping the sides of the bathtub, Saxon laid her head back and rocked her hips in rhythm to Susan's subtle but intense touch. "You're making me crazy."

As if wanting to torture her with pleasure even more, Susan used the tip of her tongue to trace the edge of Saxon's ear. The touch was cool, and more sensuous than Saxon could have imagined. Combined with the finger pressing on her clit, Saxon felt a heat rising in her. A thunder starting from her core. She had never felt anything like it, and her body began to tighten. "You're so close," Susan whispered into her ear. "And I'm your first."

"This feels so incredible..." Saxon answered as the climax started to roll over her like a wave. "Oh, God, what is happening?"

Susan slipped a finger inside her at the exact moment Saxon's world exploded, and she felt like her entire body was melting from the intensity of the orgasm. "You're coming, darling," Susan assured her. "Let all of it take you."

Saxon shook, splashing a bit of water over the tub's side as she cried out over and over in pleasure. Nothing she ever imagined felt like what was happening to her. As Susan pulled out to let her relax, Saxon knew she never wanted it to end.

11

Pulling into the L-shaped driveway, Saxon stopped the car outside the garage to think. Faye sat in the passenger seat beside her. Neither said anything during the twenty-minute drive up the coast as if both had been lost in their thoughts about what may lay ahead. The highway from Santa Monica to Malibu followed the Pacific Coast. There was a perfect view of the quarter moon reflecting on the inky black of the ocean. Cold, white light from it spread like a carpet over the waves, speckled here and there with a hint of movement as a whitecap rolled over. But then they were at Saxon's home, and she needed to decide—invite Faye into the house or turn the car around to take her home.

"Was this okay?" Saxon finally asked, with a hint of a laugh. "Perhaps I should have asked that question earlier."

Faye looked at her. "It's okay," she said, taking off her seatbelt and leaning closer to Saxon. "Are you all right with it now that we are here?"

Saxon was, but then again, she wasn't. So many years had passed since she was alone with a woman she wanted to touch so badly. But there was no way of knowing where

71

things might lead if Saxon followed her instincts. She knew she wasn't ready to disclose details about her past, both recent and a century ago. Faye was nearly a stranger. There was no way to know how she would react if the truth came out. Even though Saxon felt like she trusted her to be open-minded, a person could never tell what might happen. People could be a surprise. All those thoughts raced through Saxon's mind while Faye waited for an answer. Turning around and taking Faye back to pick up her car was the smartest thing to do, but the last thing she wanted. "I am glad you are here," Saxon admitted. "But maybe we should start with a walk on the beach?"

"Hmmm," Faye murmured. "Yes, that sounds nice. The weather is ideal and warm, even for a night in November."

"Perfect," Saxon said, getting out of the car. Faye did the same, and together they took the dozen wooden steps down the short cliff to the sand below. Slipping off her black Converse and socks because she loved the feel of the sand between her toes, Saxon sighed. "I love it down here. Especially in the moonlight."

"Do you walk the beach often?" Faye asked, removing her brown, low-heel boots and then her socks, before glancing at the house above. "And your home looks gorgeous. So many windows facing the ocean."

Once Faye was ready, they started walking toward the tideline where the sand was firmer. "Yes. Thank you," Saxon said. "Living near the ocean is such a nice change. I'd forgotten how much it spoke to me."

Out of the corner of her eye, Saxon saw Faye tilt her head and look at her. She mentally kicked herself for sharing anything. Already the actress looked curious, and questions had to be coming soon. "I love the ocean too," Faye said, surprising Saxon a little. She really was expecting a barrage of questions. "Maybe I should move out here somewhere. Although it might be hard to keep the paparazzi out."

Saxon pursed her lips. "Where do you live now?" she asked, and Faye smiled.

"Beverly Hills, of course," she answered and laughed. "Buying a fancy house there was what my agent recommended." Then, she sobered. "But the place sits behind a high gate and even higher walls."

"And you hate that part," Saxon said. The sentence wasn't a question, but Faye nodded anyway.

"I do. Don't get me wrong," she said. "I have a wonderful life. Extremely fortunate. But sometimes..." They walked a few steps in silence. Saxon didn't pry. Faye would tell her the rest of what she was feeling, or she wouldn't. "...sometimes I just wish I could disappear and start all over again." She stopped and met Saxon's eyes. "Do you understand?"

Saxon smiled a little. "I do."

Faye stared into Saxon's eyes, so dark but with a little shine from the moonlight reflecting in them. Even though the woman smiled, there was a touch of melancholy to the tone of her answer. She spoke like someone so much older than she looked. As if she had traveled the world already and seen a lifetime of things, but that was impossible. "How old are you?" Faye blurted, then covered her mouth with her hand. "Oh my God, that's the rudest question. I can't believe I just asked you that. I'm so sorry."

Saxon laughed and started walking again. "Forget it," she said. "Let's just say I'm much older than I look." Faye could live with that, and for a while they strolled in silence. The moonlit night was perfect with the sound of gentle waves running up the shore, and there was no one around to bother them. She thought maybe she could walk forever, but then Saxon slowed their steps. "We should turn back. I think we've come farther than we realize."

Looking around, Faye agreed. She was not sure where she even was and doubted she could find Saxon's home again. "You're right," she said, starting to turn when Saxon reached out a hand to touch her face. Her fingers were cool, yet heat flushed to Faye's face at the contact. There was a spark between them that made her heart race. Her eyes dropped to the woman's lips, full and so kissable. Her heart racing, she didn't know what to do next but wished Saxon would say or do something.

After a pause, Saxon leaned in until their mouths were less than an inch apart. "Do you have any idea how attracted I am to you?" she whispered, and Faye felt a tingle run through her. "When I kissed you in your trailer, I thought I might go crazy if I couldn't have more of you. That knock at the door..."

Faye slipped her arms around Saxon's shoulders. "Me too," she said, still unable to look away from her mouth. "No one's ever kissed me like that."

"Good," Saxon said and closed the distance between them. Her lips met Faye's—strong, possessive—and she moved her hands to Faye's hips to pull her close. Body against body, Faye could not hold back a moan. Desire coursed through her, and when Saxon pushed her lips apart to take her mouth, her body began to ache for more.

Breathless, she pulled back and studied Saxon's face. "God, how did you learn to kiss like that?" she asked. "It's amazing."

Leaning her forehead against Faye's, Saxon chuckled.

"I've had a little practice," she said. "But thank you. To be fair, it takes two to kiss like that."

"I see," Faye said. "Then let's do it again." At her request, Saxon didn't hesitate and kissed her, even more passionately than the last. Their mouths moved against each other, filled with want, and Faye needed more. As if reading her mind, Saxon broke the kiss to move her lips up Faye's cheek to her ear.

"Let's go back," she whispered, and Faye nodded. Slipping apart a little, Saxon took her hand, and together they walked toward the house. As they went, Faye's cellphone began to ring, and she felt conflicted. Her number was private so only a close friend or family member would be calling. Before she could decide, Saxon motioned toward the sound coming from her back pocket.

"It's okay with me," she said. "In case the call is important."

Reaching for her phone, she gave the woman a grateful smile. "The number is private, so not too many people have —" She stopped midsentence when she saw the screen. Unknown Caller. A cold ball formed in the bottom of her stomach because she knew the call was from her stalker. He'd been quiet since the note delivered by the gate guard. That message was short but frightening. *"I've been thinking of you."* Still, Faye had yet to go to the police. A record of the problem would undoubtedly be leaked to a reporter at some point, and she didn't want that kind of publicity.

Saxon stopped. "What's wrong?" she asked, and when Faye glanced up from her phone, she saw legitimate concern on the woman's face. "You have a stalker." Again, not a question and Saxon frowned. "Do you want me to answer it for you?"

Faye thought that through for a moment but then

nodded as she handed the phone over to Saxon. "Just to make sure I'm not crazy," she said. The movie director answered, and Faye watched her face grow hard as she listened. The call was clearly from the asshole bothering her. After another few seconds of listening, Saxon hung up and looked at Faye. Her face was so dark with anger, Faye's instinct was to step back. There was something scary about Saxon at this moment, but then she seemed to recover with a shake of her head.

Handing the phone back, Saxon retook her hand and started them walking. "Have you taken this to the police?" she asked, and Faye explained why she hadn't. Saxon frowned but seemed to accept the answer. "I will ensure we make the movie sets safe, but I suggest you hire some personal security. You haven't heard the last of this man." Faye swallowed hard at the chilling words.

"I need you, and you need me," the stalker had said through the phone. Then nothing but heavy breathing until Saxon hung up. The words were chilling, and she sensed madness in his tone. She also picked up on his determination, and that was what worried her the most. Faye was in real danger, and every instinct to protect her flared up inside Saxon. Somehow, she would have to keep her safe, but doing so would be difficult when separated. For the moment though, Faye was beside her, and she wanted to keep her there.

"What did he say?" Faye asked as they walked faster toward Saxon's home.

Saxon shook her head. "That doesn't matter," she said. "What he said was just meant to scare you."

Faye pulled her to a stop. "Tell me," she insisted. "I have a right to know."

Saxon clenched her jaw in frustration but knew the woman was right. He said, "I need you, and you need me." She watched Faye's face pale in the moonlight. She dropped Saxon's hand and put them to her cheeks.

"Oh my God," she whispered. "What should I do? Nothing like this has ever happened. I get some weird fan mail, but this..."

Saxon took her by the arm and started them moving again even faster than before. "Let's get back to my house," she said. She wasn't concerned about their safety, but there was no way to explain that fact to Faye. For now, she only wanted them to be inside rather than exposed on the beach. Before long, they were racing up the steps and ducking through the sliding glass door into her home. Saxon led her to the great room so Faye could sit and gather herself. Unfortunately, Louis stepped out of the kitchen, and when Faye saw him, she screamed.

"It's okay," Saxon said, reaching to pull her into an embrace. The woman did not resist and wrapped her arms around Saxon's neck. She felt her trembling. "He's my friend, and he lives here."

Louis was standing with his hands clasped together, dismay on his face. "I had no idea someone was with you," he said, his voice shaking.

"There was no way for you to know," Saxon said, still holding Faye and frustrated with herself. The night had been such a whirlwind; she'd been careless. "I should have sent a text. Please, everyone, try to relax." She looked into Faye's face. "You are safe here. More than you can imagine."

Faye bit her lip but slowly relaxed her grip, and the shaking stopped. "I'm sorry," she said. "I didn't mean to scream. It's just, after the call."

Saxon kissed her forehead. "You were acting on

instinct," she said. "This is my fault. Louis, please make sure the house is secure and set the alarm."

The man gave her a nod. "Yes, of course," he said and then left them alone.

"Thank you so much," Faye said. "But you don't need to protect me, and I'm putting you in danger by being here. I should go."

"I am not afraid. I promise we are safe here. You can stay with me for now," Saxon said and then realized how that sounded. She hated the idea of letting Faye out of her sight but had to give her a choice. "I mean, I have a guest room if you want to use it."

"No," Faye said with a small shake of her head.

"No?" Saxon repeated, unsure of what she was meaning.

Faye hugged her tighter. "No to the guest room. I want to be with you," she said. "Somehow, you make me feel incredibly safe."

12

"Everything is secure," Louis said after returning to the great room to rejoin them. "I moved your car into the garage as well."

Faye let out a breath of relief she didn't even know she had been holding. Still feeling anxious over everything, she was glad to hear they were safe. Saxon smiled from beside her where they sat together on the large, tan suede sectional in the great room. She had snuggled under a matching throw blanket and leaned her head against Saxon's shoulder. Usually, she hung proudly to her independence, but tonight she was happy to have someone to take care of her. "Thank you, Louis," Saxon said. "Perhaps we should make introductions?"

Louis gave a half bow. "It is my pleasure to meet you, ma'am," he said, and Faye raised her eyebrows at the formality. For a second, she wasn't sure if he was playing, but then realized he was completely serious. She glanced at Saxon, who shrugged a shoulder.

"Louis is my personal assistant," she said with an awkward little laugh. "But sometimes kind of like a butler."

Faye turned back to him. "It's my pleasure too," she said. "I'm sorry I overacted when I saw you earlier."

"It's my fault. I shouldn't have stepped out of nowhere without saying something first," he said. "Can I get you anything to drink? Wine? Or something stronger?"

Wine sounded divine to Faye, and she nodded. "I'd love a glass," she said. "A big glass."

"I'll help you with the wine selection, Louis," Saxon said before looking at Faye. "Are you okay alone for a minute?"

Although a part of her wasn't keen on being away from Saxon for even a second, Faye nodded. Still, she needed to get a grip on her fear, so put on a brave face. "I'm fine," she lied. "But I don't need anything fancy."

Saxon leaned in and kissed her on the forehead. "I'll be right back," she said, standing and walking to follow her assistant down the hall to what Faye assumed was a wine cellar. As soon as she was out of sight, Faye felt her chest tighten with anxiety. For some reason, the fright Louis gave her brought home the reality of all of it. The threats were real, and her stalker knew a lot about her. Too much. She racked her brain to think if there was anyone she knew who could be doing this to her, but her circle was small, and she had always worked hard to keep her personal life private. With a sigh, she accepted the reality she would need to tell the police and hire security. At least for tonight though, she could stay with Saxon.

The thought of sleeping beside her moved Faye's feelings of anxiety more toward tingles of desire. She wondered what Saxon's bedroom would look like and if they would do more than sleep. Looking around the room, the furnishings were tasteful, expensive, but rather generic. Almost as if she hired a designer to stage the place before she moved in. The house was gorgeous. Under different circumstances, she would love to go out on the expanse of the balcony that surrounded most of the house. But not tonight. She only wanted to be inside, burrowed down, trying to feel safe.

Being on Saxon's couch helped, and when the woman sat beside her, Faye never felt more protected. Even though Saxon wasn't taller than Faye's five-foot-seven, she gave off a more significant presence. Faye knew she had a lean body that felt hard with muscle from their tight embraces, but that did not explain the power she radiated. The confidence. As if she were unstoppable. Faye realized those qualities drew her, part of their chemistry, and certainly explained her instant attraction. An attraction that made her shiver as she thought about where things could lead tonight. The vision of Saxon on top of her made Faye suck in a breath. A dull throb started between her legs, and she loved the distraction from her other fears. This was what she needed tonight. Saxon was what she needed.

Picking a simple California blend, Saxon was eager to go back to Faye. Although she was entirely safe here, she knew the actress was anxious and needed reassurances. "I'm sorry about what happened," Louis apologized again.

Saxon waved him off. "I should have alerted you," she said and smiled. "She's lovely, isn't she?"

Louis nodded. "Indeed," he said and then turned quiet. Saxon sensed his hesitation but waited for him to say what was on his mind rather than press. "Does she know?"

"No," Saxon said, knowing this could present a bit of a problem. "I'll just have to control myself if things go that far." She walked back to the stairs with the wine while Louis hung back as his suite of rooms was on the ground level.

"Goodnight," he said. "Enjoy your evening. If you need anything, please let me know."

"Thank you. Goodnight," Saxon said and then jogged up the stairs, speaking before she rushed into the great room to avoid surprising Faye. "I'll have this open in a minute." The woman was still snuggled under the blanket, but her eyes looked damp, and Saxon paused to set the wine on an end table rather than go into the kitchen. As she went toward her, Faye pushed the blanket aside and reached out her arms. Saxon sunk into them. "Hey, I shouldn't have left you. It's okay now."

"I'm sorry," Faye whispered, wrapping her arms around her neck. "This is not how I usually act."

Saxon held her. "This has been a scary night," she said, hating the thought Faye might blame herself for any of what had happened. They sat quietly for a moment, and Saxon was unsure what to do next other than let Faye take the lead. If she wanted, she would sit with her on the couch all night.

"Thank you for being so understanding," Faye finally said, lifting her face to look into Saxon's. "You're my hero." Saxon smiled, loving her words. Being Faye's hero was all she could want, and when the time came that she found the stalker... Pushing all anger aside, Saxon put a hand on Faye's cheek. Moving nearer until their mouths were close enough, she felt Faye's hot breath on her lips. The desire to kiss her was suddenly all consuming, yet she respected the woman may no longer be feeling passionate.

"Do you still want wine?" she whispered. "Or something to eat?"

In answer, Faye closed the distance until their mouths collided. Saxon was surprised at the hunger in the woman's kiss but then focused on nothing but their lips together. The heat was intense and sent shivers through her. She loved the warmth against her. Moving on instinct, she broke the kiss to pull Faye closer, turning her so she straddled Saxon's lap. Their mouths met again, and a moan escaped Faye when Saxon pressed forward with her tongue, searching, wanting. When she parted her lips, the flame of need inside her roared into a fire threatening to consume her. She wanted this woman more than she had wanted anyone in a very long time.

"Take me to your bedroom," Faye whispered as she moved her mouth and ran her lips along Saxon's jaw. A nip at her earlobe, and there was nothing that would stop her from obeying the request. She stood from the couch, lifting Faye with her effortlessly. The sudden show of strength made Faye gasp. "God, you are strong."

Saxon chuckled. "I work out," she said, and as Faye wrapped her legs around her waist, she carried her to the master bedroom suite. Another passionate kiss in the doorway made the ache in Saxon only grow stronger. As she kicked the door closed behind her, she reminded herself Faye was delicate. And mortal.

Saxon was so many things. Sexy, sensual, brave, and incredibly strong. Faye felt like a feather in her arms, and when she lay her back gently onto the bed, she felt safer than ever. For a moment, Saxon gazed at her with eyes reflecting black in the moonlight coming in through the window. Her expression was one of desire. Never had Faye felt more wanted than when she looked into the woman's face. "You are so desirable, Faye Stapleton," Saxon whispered as she lowered herself onto the bed. They fell into another kiss, this one even more passionate than the other. Feeling heat building in her body, Faye moaned, and she grabbed Saxon's shirt to pull it off.

"You are the one who's desirable," she said, her voice husky with lust. "And I want you naked." Not resisting, the shirt came off, and then Saxon unfastened her belt. The sight made Faye squirm, and she reached to help. In response, Saxon's freed hands pulled at Faye's buttons. Suddenly, it was a race to see who could undress the other first.

In a rush of excitement, their clothing was tossed to the floor, and Saxon pushed Faye's legs apart before slipping her body between them. The woman's tight abs slid across Faye's folds, pressing down on her clit, and her hips lifted in response. An orgasm threatened already, and she felt amazement at how turned on she was. Running her hands down Saxon's back, she grabbed her, pulling her hard against the throbbing need building between her legs. As if on instinct, Saxon began to thrust against her, rubbing their clits together. Faye felt her own dripping wetness smearing between them as her breath came faster.

Running her hands up Faye's body, Saxon cupped one of her breasts and guided the tip to her waiting mouth. With a sudden gentle bite, Faye let out a small cry of surprise as a bolt of pain and pleasure shot through her. Then, Saxon began to lick and tickle before sucking on it long and slow in rhythm to the thrusting of her hips against Faye. The mixture of sensations was unbelievable, and Faye tilted her head back into the pillow to relish the pleasure. "You feel incredible," she moaned as Saxon moved to the other breast. Another nip, and even though Faye anticipated the shock, her body shook at the sensation, and she nearly tipped over into her climax. Only willpower to make it last kept her from coming, but she couldn't stand much more.

Saxon slid up her body a little and took her mouth in another burning kiss. Her insistent tongue conquered Faye's mouth with so much hunger that she whimpered. Their bodies continued to rock against each other, and when Saxon moved her hand down between them, Faye could not have been more ready. "I want to take you," Saxon growled into her mouth, and the words made her feel like she was melting from the heat inside her.

"I want that," she panted, and in response Saxon slid her fingers lower until they slipped through Faye's wetness and between her lips. Circling her clit for a moment, Faye tried to squirm, but Saxon was in complete control and pressed her tight into the mattress. She couldn't escape if she tried. Then, Saxon's fingers were inside her in a stroke that stretched Faye and made her suck in a breath. The sensation of being controlled, as if she had no choice but to let go, made Faye wild. No other lover had been like this with her. They were tentative and overly gentle, but power radiated off Saxon's body. The woman's fingers stroked her in and out, sliding deeper with every thrust. The feeling of being so taken was too much to control, and in a rush, the orgasm she tried to hold back overwhelmed her. "Oh Saxon, I'm coming."

At that moment, Saxon lifted on one arm and looked down into her face, and for a second, the moonlight reflecting in Saxon's eyes made them red. Before Faye made sense of it, the color was gone, and she abandoned herself to the waves of incredible pleasure rolling over her.

13

LOS ANGELES, PRESENT DAY

Listening to the waves crash onto the beach below, Saxon sat back in a patio lounger and gazed at the midnight stars overhead. The night sky was cloudless and as she watched, a shooting star drew a thin line across the heavens for a moment and then was gone. On a whim, she closed her eyes and made a wish. She knew the request would be unlikely, but her mood was good tonight after her time with Faye. With a sigh, she opened her eyes again and let them drift to Andromeda. Then, Cassiopeia. Over the years, she'd memorized the many constellations. When you never slept, there was plenty of time to learn things.

Tonight though, her mind was on Faye, who slept naked in her king-sized bed. At first the woman was restless, but Saxon held her until she fell into a deep sleep. Then, she slipped away silently to come outside and think, knowing she would return to the woman's side soon. The last thing she wanted was for Faye to wake up alone in a strange place. But Saxon needed a moment to gather herself. The lure of the woman's scent and the vibrant sound of her heartbeat were powerful. She struggled to be so close to her. Their chemistry was strong, too strong, and Saxon was having trouble getting her feelings in check. When Faye climaxed, Saxon wanted to change and nearly did, but the actress was far from ready for that information.

Over the decades, Saxon had many lovers who never knew what she was, but those were always short affairs, often only one-night stands and based purely on carnal attraction. Some she had bitten and fed from as she climaxed but was careful not to turn them. Sneaking away in the night afterward, she would leave them weak and disoriented but alive. Not until Faye had her attraction been enough that she brought the woman to her home, her sanctuary. Rubbing a hand over her face, she was not sure why she'd spontaneously done it. There was something different about her. The desire was incredible between them, and their sex was fantastic. She also made Saxon feel things she hadn't since the beginning. Real, raw emotions that caught her by surprise, and nothing concerned her more. Saxon wasn't certain this was what she wanted.

The best answer at the moment seemed to be to put emotional distance between them and try to start over again with only a friendship. Keeping their relationship professional was the right thing to do, for the rest of the film at least. Perhaps by then, the flames burning between them would have cooled, and Saxon could get her head on straight. Grinding her teeth in frustration, she had a feeling the heat between her and Faye would not just go away.

As she got off the lounger, Saxon shook her head at the idea of backing away from Faye. Especially when someone was stalking her. The protective instinct in Saxon flared at even the thought of a person trying to hurt her. For some strange reason, she felt responsible for Faye's safety. As if their meeting through this film was predestined. There was only one problem—how could she keep her safe from the man who stalked her while keeping her safe from Saxon's desires too?

Blinking her eyes open, Faye had no idea where she was, and her chest tightened with anxiety. Looking around the sparsely furnished bedroom, it felt like a room where no one spent much time, and that scared her. The thought of her stalker's messages came flooding in, and then she saw Saxon sitting in a chair beside the bed. A mug of hot coffee steamed on the nightstand beside her. "Good morning," she said, her tone gentle and caring. "Everything is okay. You're safe here."

The words relaxed Faye immediately, and she smiled. "Thank you," she said, reaching to take Saxon's hand and pull her onto the bed. "You make me feel safe." New memories rushed in to replace the bad ones. She imagined Saxon's hands on her again, stroking her, making her come, and she shivered with pleasure. Another round of that attention would be a great way to start the morning, yet Saxon seemed hesitant and did nothing but sit on the edge of the bed. Even her hand felt cool. Faye frowned. "What's wrong?"

For a moment, Saxon did nothing but look at their hands clasped together, and then she let her eyes drift up to meet Faye's. "I've just been thinking things through," she said. "A lot about the call from the stalker and how to keep you safe. Do you want me to postpone filming for a few days? Until we can get the best possible security in place?"

Faye sat up in the bed, scooching back to rest her back against the headboard. She pulled the sheet up to cover her breasts, suddenly feeling a little self-conscious. Saxon's answer didn't feel right, but the fact she worried about Faye's safety made sense. She wasn't sure quite what to think, other than she did not want to force the film off schedule. People's careers counted on things flowing smoothly when a big-budget movie was at stake. The last thing Faye wanted was to be a disruption. "No," she said with a shake of her head. "I don't want to do that. There's no way I'm letting this asshole intimidate me that much."

Nodding, Saxon gave her hand a squeeze and then let go as she stood. "We'll beef up security on the location tonight," she said, a hint of detachment in her voice. "And I'll help you arrange for personal protection. But until it's in place, I'd like you to stay here."

The awkward feeling between them only seemed to be getting worse. "Saxon, what is going on?" she asked. "Did I do something wrong?"

At that, Saxon's face softened, and sadness filled her eyes. "No," she replied. "I promise. This is all my fault, and I owe you an apology."

"For what?" Faye asked, furrowing her brow in confusion. "You've been nothing but wonderful." She felt a blush climbing her cheeks as she thought of Saxon on top of her. "Amazing actually."

She saw Saxon swallow hard and avert her eyes to look out the window. "I took advantage of you last night," she murmured. "You were upset and wanted comfort, but I crossed a line." Clenching her jaw, clearly frustrated, she returned her look to Faye's face. "We need to keep our relationship professional. I want you to stay here. It's important to me that you're protected, but in the guest room." All Faye did was blink she was so surprised. After last night, it was impossible that Saxon felt that way. Nothing could be further than how Faye interpreted their time together. She certainly hadn't taken advantage of her. Before she could say anything, Saxon went on, apparently taking Faye's lack of response as acknowledgment. "When you're ready, I'll take you to your house so you can pack some things." Then, without letting Faye answer, she turned and left the room.

Driving down Sunset Boulevard toward the neighborhood of Beverly Hills, Saxon wished she knew a way to make Faye understand. Unfortunately, that was difficult. Trying to explain there were elements of danger to being in a passionate relationship with Saxon was impossible. So, they rode in silence, and she tried to ignore Faye's look of shifting emotions—hurt, fury, confusion.

When the car's GPS showed they were making the last turn before reaching Faye's estate, the woman turned in her seat to pin Saxon with a glare. "I don't need to stay with you," she said. "Frankly, I'm overreacting to all of this. Somehow the creep has my phone number, and I don't know how that happened, but I'll just get a new one."

Saxon frowned, not liking this new resistance and frustration curled up in her. There was no chance she would agree to leave Faye behind. Not before the best security was in place, and even then, perhaps not. She clearly recalled the stalker's voice on the phone last night. Chilling. Serious. Determined. He did not sound like someone who would be deterred by a changed phone number. "Faye, I know you're upset with me—" Saxon started.

Faye barked a laugh to cut her off. "Upset?" she said with raised eyebrows. "I'm more than upset over this. You've suddenly taken it upon yourself to decide what's right for us. As if I don't have a say in the matter."

Surprised by the words, but knowing she was right, Saxon glanced into the woman's snapping hazel eyes. She hated how all of this was being perceived. "You don't under-stand," she said, but knowing there was nothing she could say to make the situation better.

"Then explain it to me. Please," Faye responded, more hurt than anger in her tone this time. "Just be honest with me."

Saxon stared out the windshield. What she was asking was easier said than done. As she tried to think of some-thing that didn't sound like a lame brushoff, they rounded the corner to Faye's wide driveway. As Saxon slowed, she noticed the estate's gate was open. Faye seemed to realize it at the same time. "This isn't right. Something has happened." There was no doubt in Saxon's mind the open gate connected to the stalker's threats, and she stopped the car. "Why are you stopping? I want to see what is going on."

"We need to wait and call the police," Saxon said, while every instinct in her wanted to leap out of the car and see if the man was still on the premises somewhere. Hunting him would be her pleasure.

Faye started to get out of the car. "I'm going to my house," she said. "With or without you." Saxon reached and took her by the hand. There was no way she was going to let Faye out of her sight.

"I'll drive you," she said, and when Faye relaxed back into the seat, she drove them up the long driveway. Things did not improve as they pulled up to the front of the house. Faye's front door was wide open.

Faye covered her mouth with her hand. "Oh my God," she said with a quiver in her voice. "Someone's been here."

"Stay in the car," Saxon said. "And lock the doors after I get out."

This time it was Faye's turn to grab Saxon. "Are you

kidding?" she said. "You can't do this by yourself. We really do need to call the police."

Saxon paused, not ready to argue. Getting out of the car to see if she detected any trace of the intruder was not something to negotiate on. For all she knew, the predator could still be in the house. She hoped he was if she could get Faye to stay put.

Saxon opened her door. "I will be all right," she said, gently pulling away from Faye's grasp. "I know how to defend myself, and this will only take a minute." Before the woman said another word, Saxon was out of the car and closing the door before moving toward the house's wide-open French double front door. Sniffing the air for a human scent and listening for any unusual sounds, she slipped inside. Four quick steps took her across the empty foyer to the expanse of the living room, and she froze. What she saw made her anger turn red hot, and the desire to change rose in her. She would hunt this man.

Suddenly, she heard a sound behind her and whirled around in a crouch only to find Faye standing at the entrance to the living room. Her face was pale, and her frightened eyes were locked on the white wall behind Saxon. Over the fireplace, written with something red, in two-foot-high letters, was one sentence. "Where are you?"

14

Thankful her hands finally stopped shaking, Faye sat on her best friend's couch, under a fleece blanket with a superhero logo, and drank a sip of chamomile tea. She was grateful to have a place of refuge, at least for the moment, although she had already explained to Jane she wouldn't stay with them past today. Faye felt the risk to the family's safety was too high, and she was only there because Jane's husband was off work today and home. She believed things would be okay while he was here, considering he was a six-foot-four police officer.

Still, if she had to admit it, she'd rather be with Saxon. No matter what the woman said this morning, Faye wanted to be near her. Not just because of the amazing attraction that drew her in, but because she felt incredible safe. Saxon simply radiated power, especially after they saw the message on the wall. All but carrying Faye out, she helped her into the car and took her to Jane's. Unfortunately, Saxon needed to leave to secure the movie location tonight and arrange for someone to fetch Faye's car. Checking her Apple watch, Faye saw it was thirty minutes until Saxon would be back to pick her up. She was anxious to go not only to see her but to stop worrying she was putting Jane and her family in harm's way.

After turning on a movie for the boys in the TV room, Jane returned to sit beside Faye. She put an arm around her shoulders and pulled her into a side hug. "You're sure you don't want something a little stronger than tea?" Jane asked. "I'm fairly sure we have some rum left from our last party. I could mix it with a diet coke?"

Faye rested her head on Jane's shoulder. "No, thanks," she said. "I need to be sharp for the shoot tonight, and Saxon will be here soon."

"Are you sure you're up for that tonight?" Jane asked. "I can't imagine they wouldn't take a night off for you after this."

Faye lifted her head and pulled the blanket up higher. "No, Saxon already offered me that," she said. "But I'm not going to let this guy jeopardize my chance on being in *Venandi*. It means too much to me."

Jane nodded. "Okay," she said. "But if you see anything or start to feel weird—"

"I will stop," Faye interrupted with a weak smile. "I promise."

"And you're sure you don't want to stay with us a little longer?" Jane asked. "Mitch will stay home another day or two if it will make you feel better."

Faye snaked a hand from under the blanket and grabbed Jane's. She gave it a squeeze. The woman was such a good friend, and Faye knew she was lucky to have her in her life. Which was even more reason she would never agree to stay longer than she already had. If anything happened to them, she would never be able to forgive herself. "No," she answered. "I love you guys, and Mitch is a saint for being willing to do that, but I'll be staying with Saxon."

Jane raised her eyebrows. "Saxon?" she asked. "I just assumed you were going to a hotel with extra security." She leaned in closer to keep her voice at a whisper. "Are you two sleeping together?" Faye felt her cheeks go pink, and Jane sat back, covering her mouth with her hands. "Oh my God, you are."

"It's not what you think," Faye said. "I mean, we did have a great time last night, even with the creep's call, but now I don't know what is going on between us."

"What do you mean?" Jane asked looking confused, and Faye gave her a quick play-by-play of the morning's conversation. Blinking with surprise, Jane was quiet for a moment before shaking her head. "That's confusing as hell."

"Tell me about it," Faye said when Mitchell, Jr., the eldest of Jane's boys, ran into the room.

"Mom, look out the window," he said, excitement dancing in his eyes. "The coolest black car just got here."

Jane frowned. "I thought you were watching a movie, not looking out the windows." Mitchell, Jr. suddenly became interested in his socks as if he hadn't heard her, and Jane sighed. "Back in the TV room, buster." As the boy ran off, Jane stood. "Let me guess. Batwoman has arrived to rescue you?" Faye laughed off her comment, but inside she agreed. Somehow, she thought Saxon could very well be a superhero.

Walking the area around the rundown East LA neighborhood location where they were filming, Saxon used all her senses to see if she felt a predator nearby. Considering they were at the edge of known gang territory, she expected to pick up on something, but so far, there was nothing. She would do everything she could to keep things that way. A man in a black jacket with SECURITY stenciled in white on the back gave her a nod as she turned the corner to head back to where the cameras were setting up. The security company she hired last minute came highly recommended. She was pleased with her manager's response when Saxon asked her to help arrange things. Courtney was even onsite tonight as if her presence would help calm the situation. She knew as well as anyone that having word get out that a stalker was bothering Faye could derail the movie. Paparazzi would be everywhere. It was Courtney's job as much as anyone's to make sure that didn't happen, including making sure Saxon didn't get too distracted over it.

Rejoining the film crew, Saxon watched Courtney walk over, not a hair out of place, dressed in another stylish business suit. The woman raised an eyebrow. "Well?" her manager said. "Feeling better about things?"

Saxon let her eyes scan the area as she answered. "Not really. But Faye insists we move ahead with this scene. I will respect her wishes and do all I can to make sure she is safe."

Courtney tilted her head as she regarded Saxon. "You seem especially invested in Faye Stapleton," she said after a beat. "Something I should know about?"

Saxon shrugged. "She's the star of my movie."

The woman narrowed her eyes. The answer clearly didn't satisfy her manager's curiosity. "Yes," she said. "That's true. But I am feeling something else here."

"Let it go," Saxon said, her voice a little harsher than she intended. Before she could smooth it over, the second assistant director waved at them while he jogged over.

"Ms. Stapleton's on her way from hair and makeup," the man said. Saxon felt mixed emotions churn in her at the idea of seeing Faye, even though they rode over to the location together not two-hours before. The ride had been subdued, almost awkward until Saxon couldn't take the distance between them any longer and reached to take Faye's hand. Faye held on tight, and she knew the woman felt more frightened than she was letting on. Still, any conversation about not filming tonight met with complete resistance. At last the time was here they could start and get the night over with. She wanted Faye safely back at her home in Malibu where Saxon could ensure no harm would come to her.

"Let everyone know to get ready. I want this to run smoothly tonight," Saxon said while noticing Brad Norris, ready for filming, starting to argue with the production assistant assigned to him. That was the last thing she needed. The actor was pivotal in this scene as he and Faye had a direct conversation. If he decided to be difficult, the night could take forever. Walking in their direction, Saxon overheard the heated discussion. Apparently, the lead actor had misgivings about taking his mark before Faye. Typical posturing in the business to determine who was the top dog in the movie.

"Is she even here yet?" Brad growled as Saxon reached them. He turned on Saxon. "Because I'm not just going to stand around like some two-bit B-Actor." She didn't say a word as their eyes met. In an instant, she knew this man was weak, and although he had the reputation of being a big seducer of women, it was his handsome looks that did the work, not his passion. There was no hunt in him. Her gaze sent off quite the opposite, and Brad could only hold her look for a second. His already pale face from makeup turning even more so as he backed away. Mumbling an apology, he slunk to his mark and waited.

· · ·

Flanked by two sizeable men in black windbreakers, Faye felt relatively safe walking from the hair and makeup trailer to where they were filming. The possibility seemed unlikely that her stalker would try anything out in the open, but Saxon was taking no chances. Still, it wasn't until she saw the movie director standing at the edge of the lights illuminating the scene that she felt her body relax. Confident, sexy, clearly in charge, Saxon Montague. Last night, when they walked on the beach and kissed, Faye felt like the moment was magic. When Saxon touched her later that night, driving her wild with her fingertips, making her come so hard, she thought they had a real connection. Yet, Saxon implied otherwise. Living together would be next to impossible if Saxon intended for them to be only friends. Unfortunately, today's mixed messages were making it hard to focus, which was going to be a problem if she didn't get into character. This was a simple yet pivotal sequence where she first came face to face with the vampire without knowing it.

In the scene, it would be the middle of the night when Faye's character, Agent Kolchak, walked down the front stairs of a rundown apartment complex. Stepping into an area marked off with yellow police tape to keep the onlookers back, she would join the on-scene LAPD detective. Starting a discussion about what happened, Faye would look over the woman's shoulder, making eye contact with Brad's character, the vampire. He would be dressed in all black to stand out from the crowd of curious people. Unlike Brad, they wore pajamas under tattered coats, threadbare robes, plus an assortment of other combinations. Faye would walk over to the vampire at the front of the crowd, close enough to the yellow tape it nearly touched his stomach. Suspicious, Faye would ask for his name and ID. In the end, with a cheeky grin, the vampire would deliver his line,

"Goodnight, Agent Kolchak," before he slipped away into the dark night, and not long after a bat would fly over the heads of the crowd.

Thinking through the actions and dialogue she would have to perform, Faye approached the film location's edge. Having done their duty for the moment, the security guards stood out of the way of the cameras while Faye climbed the front steps of the apartment building. She stopped at her mark, the blue painter's tape T on the ground. Mixed emotions tried to distract her as she thought about looking over her shoulder at Saxon or not. Staying in character was hard enough without seeing her. Still, something inside desperately needed that connection—to see the look in her eyes that made Faye feel she was special. Then, the opportunity to decide was lost as the first assistant director asked everyone if they were ready. He pointed directly at Faye, and she nodded. Everything else fell away as she turned into Vanessa Kolchak, vampire hunter, and heard Saxon say "Action."

15

NEW ORLEANS, 1850

Dressed in nothing but a silk robe, like Susan's but instead a white cream, Saxon followed the woman up the narrow staircase to the third floor. The sensation of the fabric against Saxon's skin was like nothing she ever felt before. Cool, smooth, and so slippery against her nipples that with each step, Saxon's excitement grew. They were tight peaks on her full breasts, and the touch only added to the constant throb between her legs. Her feeling of release in the bathtub was life changing but only awakened the passion within her. Saxon needed more, especially to touch Susan as she had been touched. There would be no end to tonight until Saxon made the beautiful, sensual woman experience the pleasure she suddenly knew existed.

At last, they arrived at a closed wooden door painted dark red. Susan stopped at the threshold and turned to Saxon. Her dark eyes were bright. All the desire Saxon felt and more reflected in the woman's delicate features. There was something almost carnal in the slow smile that spread across her face, and when she bit her lip, her teeth were especially white. For the briefest moment, a cold chill ran up Saxon's spine, and her instincts were to flee, but then it was gone, and there were only Susan and all her desires.

"Do you want to come inside my bedroom?" Susan asked, her voice huskier than before, laced with a wanting Saxon felt too. "The decision has to be your choice and yours alone."

Saxon didn't hesitate. "I want to," she answered, breathless from the excitement rushing through her. The thought of being inside such a coveted space alone with Susan made her dizzy. "Please."

Susan chuckled softly at her enthusiasm. "That is good," she said, opening the door wide to show a bedroom unlike any Saxon had seen before. "Come in." Stepping in to follow her, Saxon's eyes were wide. The first thing they were drawn to was the five-armed gold candelabra burning black candles on the mantel above the room's small fireplace. Then she noticed every surface, except the tall, high-back canopy bed, had black candles on them too. The dressing table. The nightstands. Everything combined in a seductive flickering glow around the bed at the center of the room. Saxon bite her lip as she studied the dark oak offset by the hanging net curtains of gold.

Moving to the bedside, Susan traced her hand over the scarlet velvet duvet. She seemed to study the elaborate paisley design. "Do you like it?" she asked, without looking at Saxon. "This is my most intimate space, and I don't normally bring people here." Then, she turned back to face Saxon. "But I want you. So, please, close the door and come here."

Licking her lips in anticipation, Saxon obeyed, closing the distance between them and stepping into Susan's waiting arms. "I want you too," she whispered and then couldn't stand waiting any longer. She lowered her face to

Susan's and kissed her while her hands slipped the woman's silk robe apart. Susan did not resist and opened her lips to invite Saxon's tongue in to take her mouth. With an erotic moan of lust from deep in her throat, Saxon let her fingertips graze over the cool skin of Susan's hips. When she paused, hesitant of what to do next, Susan took Saxon's hands and raised them to her breasts. Relishing the feel, she ran her thumb over each hard nipple, and when she began to caress them, the woman shivered with delight.

Breaking the kiss with a gasp, Susan released the tie of her robe, pulling at the fabric until it slid off her shoulders to the ground. Her hands returned to cover Saxon's, running her fingertips over each nipple. "I want your mouth there," Susan said, coaxing her to what she needed as she sat on the edge of the bed, pulling Saxon's head to her breast. With a rush of arousal, she responded without hesitancy, eager to please her. Always. Her reward was the feel of Susan under her tongue as she sucked and tickled, causing the woman to arch her back and hum with pleasure. "Oh, you're good at this. Do you want more?"

Saxon stopped and tilted her head to study Susan's face. "Yes," she murmured. "I want everything."

"Then kneel," the woman said, spreading her legs while running her hands into Saxon's hair to guide her. "Kiss me here." Saxon's breath caught at the idea she was about to truly taste the essence of her. Everything seemed so forbidden, which only made her want to do it more. Tentatively, but moving on instinct, Saxon ran her tongue along Susan's thigh, making her gasp. "You little tease." Smiling, loving the reaction she was getting, Saxon moved her face closer to Susan's center, letting her hot breath linger over the woman's lips. "Yes. Oh, yes. Keep going."

Saxon had to focus, her own throbbing was so intense,

and knowing what the release felt like she wanted more. But first, she wanted Susan to come. Come against her mouth to let Saxon savor her. The woman wanted it too and, with a hand in her hair, pulled Saxon's face closer. "Like this?" Saxon asked a second before she drew her tongue along Susan's folds, parting them, to dip between and linger over her clit. Susan's hips bucked at the contact, and she let out a cry of pleasure.

"Yes," she gasped. "Just like that. Suck on me, lick me, do whatever you want." Obeying her lover's wishes, Saxon moved in closer, tasting with her tongue and taking long slow pulls on the spot Susan seemed to like the most. Susan moaned and lay back on the bed. "Don't stop," was all she seemed able to say between gasps. She started to writhe on the bed, grabbing the cloth under her into fists, lifting her hips in rhythm to Saxon's pulls on her clit. After only a few minutes, she screamed, and Saxon felt the throbbing of the woman's climax under her tongue as the sensation of coming roared through Susan. Then, the woman's scream turned into another moan, but this one sounded different. The sound was low as if coming from deep inside her, and somewhere between passion and pain.

Alarmed, Saxon stood and looked down at the naked form of the woman she desired most in the world, and then her heart seemed to freeze. Susan looked different. Slowly, the woman pulled her legs under her and sat up on the bed while mesmerizing Saxon with eyes turned scarlet. Her ruby lips parted, and the white teeth, so dazzling against the red, showed fangs. Fear and fascination rippled through Saxon as she stepped back from the edge of the bed.

"Susan?" she whispered, seeing the same magnificent, dark-haired beauty the woman once was, but also the dangerous smile of a predator. Saxon's mind flashed to a memory of when she came face to face with a copperhead ready to strike. Only her quick reflexes saved her that day, and a part of her mind begged her to flee tonight. Yet, unlike with the snake, Saxon was curious what the bite would feel like as it pierced her flesh.

Licking her lips, Susan moved to all fours on the bed. "Come here," she said. "Don't you still want to fuck me, Saxon?"

A shiver ran through Saxon as she took in her words, something she never imagined but suddenly wanted more than anything. "Yes," she whispered, her mouth dry, but she was wet and throbbing between her legs.

"Then let me show you how good I can make this feel," Susan said with a smile accenting the length of her fangs. Saxon's eyes drifted to her mouth, and again, she felt the mixed impulse to flee or to join her. Seeing the hesitation, Susan moved her hips. "I'm aching for you...please." That was all it took for Saxon to go to her. She climbed onto the bed until she was behind the woman and could see from the glisten on her lips, Susan truly needed her touch. "I want your fingers inside me," Susan moaned, lifting her hips. "Do you want me?"

Her heart racing, and her entire body on fire, Saxon wanted nothing else in the world. "I do," she said at the same moment she slipped a finger inside her and reveled at the tightness as Susan cried out with ecstasy.

"Yes," she said. "God, yes. More." Saxon obeyed, and with two fingers, began to slide in and out while Susan trembled. On instinct, she took hold of the woman's long hair and pulled just enough to make the woman grind her hips in excitement. "You're so good at this. I've needed you for so long." Saxon's heart filled with pleasure hearing she was satisfying Susan, but it was not enough. She wanted to feel the woman come around her fingers, so she moved faster. Pressed deeper. Susan let out a long cry of sheer, carnal pleasure, and Saxon felt her squeeze as she came. Releasing her, Saxon thought the sound was something she could never hear enough, and as Susan rolled onto her back, she lay down beside her.

"Was that good?" she asked, hoping for praise, and Susan answered by rolling toward her and putting a hand on her cheek.

"You were divine, darling," she said a moment before running a tongue over Saxon's lips. "Now, it's my turn." With a strength that surprised Saxon, Susan pushed her onto her back and straddled her hips. She immediately started to roll them to put pressure on her clit, and Saxon shivered at the sudden tension in her body. The woman knew what she was doing perfectly, and before a minute passed, Saxon was on the edge. Susan smiled down at her. "Does that feel good?"

"Yes," was all Saxon could gasp, knowing she'd been saying that all night, but one thing felt even better than the one before it, and she couldn't get enough. "It makes me want to fuck you again."

Susan chuckled. "You have to wait, darling. This is my turn," she said as she slid a hand down between them and put her palm against Saxon's center, pressing, caressing, and making her crazy. With experienced fingers, she ran the tips in a swirl around Saxon's clit, and Saxon moaned in response. "More?" Susan raised an eyebrow, and the woman never looked more seductive, somehow the fangs making her more so.

"More," Saxon said, grabbing her hips to help her move in rhythm to her strokes. "Always more."

Susan tilted her head. "Always?" she asked, and Saxon

knew what she meant. The pleasure could go on and on. "We could be together forever…"

"I want that," Saxon whispered as the passion in her began to mount. "Will it hurt?"

Susan leaned over her, lowering her face until they were nose to nose. "For a moment is all. Do you know what you are saying?"

Saxon wasn't sure, but she nodded anyway. She knew her dismal life working the farm every day would be over. Her father and brothers would miss her help, but they would get by easily enough. No more being trapped in a small town, longing for things she would never have, living only a shell of an existence. A life with Susan in the splendor of this place held the promise of adventure and passion. Yes, she wanted that, and as the orgasm started to grow insider her, Saxon nodded. "I want to be like you," she moaned and came as Susan slid her lips along Saxon's neck. And bit her.

16

"Okay, let's wrap this up for the night," Saxon said to the camera crew after she called "Cut" to end the scene. Saxon was happy with what she saw through the viewer.

The cinematographer looked at her with raised eyebrows. "All ready?" he asked. "We've got close-ups to do."

Saxon got out of her chair, not minding his question. Ending early would put them behind schedule, but she was confident they could make it up later. That was enough for Faye tonight, whether she thought so or not. The lead actress's energy was fading fast, and Saxon wanted to get her home. "They will have to be picked up later," she said to the camera crew. "And I'll watch today's dailies in the morning." She turned to the script supervisor. "Take extra good notes, please. More than just the look of the actors tonight. Get the mood of the scene too, if you can, so we can recreate this later. I don't want to lose it."

He nodded. "I'll take lots of extra pictures. Can I get a few more of the leads before they leave?"

"A few," Saxon said, looking at where Faye stood talking

to her production assistant. As if she felt Saxon's eyes on her, Faye glanced over. Tiredness showed in her hazel eyes, but there was a spark there too. It was clear she liked seeing Saxon looking at her. If only Saxon knew what she was going to do about their relationship. Firm boundaries would be essential but keeping them was going to be hard. Extremely hard.

As the script supervisor gathered up his camera and the rest of the crew started breaking down their equipment, Saxon decided she had a little time to check with security. She wanted to make sure there were no sightings of strangers near the set. As she walked the edge of the location to find the lead security guard, she saw a familiar young woman hurrying toward her. At first, she couldn't remember who she was and then realized she was the reporter from the sound stage a few weeks ago. Saxon clenched her jaw with frustration. If this reporter could get so close to the set, there was absolutely a breakdown in security.

"Saxon," she called, using her first name like they were friends. "Wait a minute."

Knowing she should just walk away, Saxon couldn't contain her irritation at this invasion. "This is a closed set," she said. "You need to leave."

"Just one question," she said with a cheeky smile. "Why all the extra security?"

Saxon glared at her. "To keep out unwanted reporters."

The woman laughed. "Not sure I believe that," she said. "Have there been threats?" Then, her eyes widened. "Does Faye Stapleton have a stalker?"

"You need to get off my set," Saxon growled, then took a deep breath. She did not want to lose her temper tonight.

Smiling, the reporter stepped closer rather than leave like Saxon ordered. If nothing else, the reporter had guts.

"Let's make a deal," she said. "I'll keep the lid on the Faye situation if you'll honestly answer a few questions for me. About you."

Slowly, Saxon counted to ten to keep herself in check. There seemed no easy way out of the situation, but she wanted to keep Faye's business out of the headlines. "Why should I trust you?" she said through gritted teeth, and the reporter tilted her head.

"I am giving you my word," she said, and for a moment, Saxon felt like she knew this reporter from somewhere else. And that she could trust her. "So, what will it be?"

"Three questions," Saxon said with a hint of a growl. It was all Saxon would agree too. A look of surprise quickly followed by excitement, crossed the reporter's face.

"Deal," she said. "Is Saxon Montague your real name?"

"Yes."

"Hmmm," the reporter said. "Interesting, it sounds too cool to be real. But okay. Why no photographs?"

Saxon smiled wryly. "I don't photograph well," she said, seeing a member of the security team finally coming over. "Next? Last one."

The reporter narrowed her eyes. "Okay," she said. "Why did you pick Los Angeles?"

Raising an eyebrow, Saxon considered the question. "Los Angeles?" she answered as the security guard joined them to escort the reporter away. "Because I was bored."

As the eager, young script supervisor approached her, Faye watched Saxon walk away. The emotion she felt when their eyes met continued to be electrifying, even after an exhausting night of filming. Two minutes ago, all she could think about was getting back to Malibu so she could take off her shoes and lie down, but after one look at Saxon, all thoughts of sleep were gone. Even at a distance, the connection between them was so intense, and yet all the doubts remained. Though they were going to stay at her house, Faye had no idea if Saxon would turn her away. It was the last thing she wanted.

"Can I have a few pictures, Ms. Stapleton?" the script supervisor said, and Faye turned her attention to the young man. From what she could tell so far, he was good at his job, but she imagined he had higher aspirations. Not that his role on the team wasn't crucial. The job took a lot of skill to keep track of every scene's details down to the kind of shoes they were wearing. All of it was in case they needed to recreate a scene at a later date. Still, it wouldn't surprise her if he aspired to be a director himself someday. In Hollywood, almost everyone starting out was looking to move up.

"Of course," she said, giving him her full attention. "Where do you want me?"

"Right where you are is good," he said, starting to take digital photos with his camera. "I will only take a couple of minutes." Faye waited as the script supervisor moved around her to photograph her from a few different angles. He was quick and efficient and true to his word. It only took him a couple minutes. "That will do it. Thank you."

Then, he turned to Brad, who had come to join them. As the script supervisor started photographing him, the actor caught Faye's eye. "Hey," Brad said. "Don't run off. I'll walk with you." Faye swallowed a sigh of annoyance. She had security guards to come with her, so the last thing she needed was interest from Brad Norris tonight. Still, she had sensed some tension with Brad lately and didn't want anything to escalate.

"Okay," she said but still waved to her team of guards so

they would know she was about ready. Deciding that working on his ego a little tonight wouldn't hurt, she gave him her famous America's sweetheart smile. "Good work tonight. I was really convinced you were a sinister serial killer for a minute there."

Brad laughed, puffing out his chest a bit, and clearly enjoying the praise. "Oh, but don't forget, I'm a disgusting vampire too," he said, and Faye frowned, thinking over his words.

"Why do you say disgusting?" she asked. "I kind of think their life would be... well, I don't know exactly. Maybe sad?"

Brad snorted a laugh as the script supervisor finished. "Sad?" Brad said. "They are blood-sucking demons, for God's sake." He walked closer to Faye without even a glance at the young man packing up. Unimpressed, Faye ignored Brad's arrogance and nodded to the young man as he started away.

"Thank you," she said, and the script supervisor smiled as he left the two of them alone. Then she looked back at Brad, who was standing way too close, and continued her argument. "If they do drink blood, I imagine it is only to stay alive. I just don't think they are as evil as this movie makes them seem."

As if she were a child misunderstanding him, he put his hand on her elbow. "Faye," he said in a condescending tone. "First of all, there are no such things as vampires therefore this is a dumb conversation." Not liking any of that, Faye shrugged him off, and he narrowed his eyes.

"I think I'll walk back myself," Faye said, an edge to her tone. She waved the security team over. "Sorry to bore you with a dumb conversation, but I think you might be the one who is wrong. I'll see you tomorrow on the set."

Color rose on Brad's cheeks. "You know, you're a lot

bitchier than the tabloids make you out to be," he said low enough the security team arriving couldn't hear him. "And if there really are vampires, as you seem to ridiculously imagine, then there are apparently hunters to kill them. And I'm all for that."

Watching security lead the reporter away, Saxon heard dolly wheels on asphalt and turned to look. The special effects crew had packed up and were moving their gear to one of the panel trucks. Saxon sighed with resignation when she saw them. They were getting a lot of work on this film. Tonight, they conjured up a remote-controlled bat to fly over the crowd. That the audience was supposed to believe the vampire changed himself into the creature was the best part. The producers loved it. Saxon thought it was ridiculous. They had yet to shoot him rising from a coffin, but Saxon knew it was coming. Still, the shenanigans weren't the crew's fault, and Saxon gave them a wave goodnight as she passed them to go to the actor's trailers.

Faye should have been at hers by then, with security guards checking the space first and then waiting outside her door. Yet, when she looked over, Saxon was surprised to see she was talking to Brad Norris while the guards hung back. The conversation appeared to be unpleasant based on their faces. Frowning, Saxon walked through the dark to join them just in time to overhear Brad's angry line as he parted. "And if there really are vampires, as you seem to ridiculously imagine, then there are apparently hunters to kill them. And I'm all for that."

Saxon slowed her steps, wondering how Faye would react, only to smile when she heard her say, "Such a bastard." At that, she had to agree. Working with Brad

Norris proved to be a balancing act between his ego and her need for him to perform.

"I heard that," she said. Startled, Faye put her hand to her chest, and the two guards reached for their guns, all turning toward her with surprised looks on their faces. Saxon forgot how quietly she moved through the shadows and held up her hands to apologize for making such a sudden appearance. "Sorry. I didn't mean to spook you."

"Wow, you didn't make a sound," one of the guards said, relaxing his shoulders. "Not a good idea, Ms. Montague."

She nodded. "You're absolutely right. But I'd like to walk with Faye back to the trailer," she said. "Alone."

The two guards looked at each other before the bigger one shrugged. "You're the boss," he said, and Saxon moved beside Faye as the two walked away to join their departing team. When they were out of sight, she studied Faye's beautiful face.

"I hope you are all right with that," she said, realizing she should have asked her first. "I apologize for just assuming."

Reaching out to touch Saxon's arm, Faye nodded. "I feel safe with you," she said in almost a whisper as she let her fingertips linger, clearly wanting to be closer to Saxon. "I'll go with you anywhere."

17

LOS ANGELES, PRESENT DAY

Walking with Saxon to the trailers to grab her bag, all Faye thought about was what would happen between them tonight. Knowing she was in the next bedroom would be torture. She wasn't sure she would be able to stand being apart, even if all they did was hold each other. "Saxon," she finally said as they walked around the corner of her trailer, and Saxon stepped ahead to unlock the trailer door. "We need to talk about tonight. My feelings—"

Before she finished, she registered a blur of motion to her left. Someone moving fast, coming from behind them between the other trailers. She watched Saxon turn her head in alarm a split second before the attack, but she was too late.

In a flash of dark clothes and the glint of a knife, someone in a ski mask grabbed Faye by the hair. He jerked her backward until she slammed against his body. The edge of his knife pressed cold against her cheek. Opening her mouth to scream, the man hissed in her ear. "Not a sound, baby," he said. "Or I'll cut that pretty face of yours."

The word 'baby' coming from his mouth made her skin

crawl, and Faye knew precisely what was happening. Her stalker had finally made his move. All his earlier messages were chilling, but the reality of him being here, with his hand grabbing her hair, made her stomach lurch. Trembling with shock and fear, Faye did as he said and clamped her mouth shut and looked with wild eyes at Saxon, who crouched by the door, clearly ready to leap at the stalker. Glaring at the man, Faye didn't think anyone could look more menacing. Her dark eyes seemed able to bore into him.

"I suggest you let her go," Saxon said in a low voice. There was a hint of a growl underlying the words that made Faye's eyes widen. The sound was almost animal. With his face still near her ear, she heard the stalker swallow hard, but the knife stayed against her face. Wisely, he started to back away but pulled Faye with him. The man was taller than she was and too strong for her to break free. And there was the knife. She felt the thing against her cheek near her eye. If Saxon attacked, it seemed impossible Faye wouldn't get cut or worse.

"Actually, this is what's going to happen," he said, still backing slowly between the length of the trailers. "I am going to take Ms. Stapleton with me before anyone else notices, while you are going to get down on your knees, and then onto your face. I can tell you're already getting ideas." Then, Faye felt the back of the hand holding the knife slide down her cheek in a caress. "There's no reason for anyone to get hurt."

She shivered with disgust, but Saxon needed to do what he said. As afraid as she was for herself, Faye wouldn't allow anyone else to get hurt through some crazy act of heroics. Not because of her. "Please do what he says," she said in a shaking voice. "I'll be okay." Faye was sure her words were a lie by the way the man was panting against her cheek as he pulled her along, but there was no other choice. Saxon continued to hold the stare for a long moment, and Faye saw the woman shaking with rage. She looked ready to rip the man to pieces.

"You won't get away," Saxon said. "Not from me. I assure you." She took a step closer, and Faye felt the man tense and the knifepoint shift.

"Please, Saxon," Faye pleaded. Saxon was amazingly strong and no doubt fast, but the situation was impossible. At her words, Saxon looked from the attacker to her, meeting her eyes with something Faye couldn't quite read at first. Fury clearly, but something else too. Then, it registered. The look was regret. Finally, Saxon looked away, studying a spot on the ground. With a little nod, it looked like she was going to drop to her knees like the attacker demanded, but she hesitated.

"Don't be a stupid fuck," the stalker cursed. Pausing his steps, he pressed the point of the knife harder into Faye's neck. "Get on your face, or this will get ugly." To emphasize his point, he nicked Faye with the knife, and instinctively she closed her eyes while crying out more in fear than in pain. He tightened his grip on her and breathed into her face. "Shut up! What did I say—"

Suddenly, there was a low moan like someone in pain coming from Saxon's direction, making both Faye and the attacker look. Faye blinked. What she was seeing was impossible, and for a moment, she was confused. Saxon's eyes, normally dark, were red, and her teeth were bright amongst the shadowy night. With a hiss, she opened her mouth wider, and Faye saw the impossible. White fangs.

. . .

Even with rage and fear for Faye coursing through her, Saxon had herself under control. She did not want to change into a vampire. The stalker was already jumpy, and Faye would know her secret. The outcome wouldn't change anything. As hard as she would try, Saxon knew she could not close the gap between them. The man with the knife would cut Faye before she stopped him. Such a simple attack, yet effective and one that left her without many choices. Saxon hadn't been thinking about predators while she walked with Faye and missed sensing him. An oversight she would never forget.

Then, the man nicked Faye's neck, and a line of blood ran down her skin. The smell of life's essence hit Saxon like a punch in the chest. All the attraction she felt toward Faye exploded inside her. She wanted the woman before, but nothing like this. Every instinct inside her fired, and she couldn't have resisted letting the vampire out no matter how hard she tried. Sorrow mixed with fury as she felt the transformation come over her. There would be no going back with Faye after this, and she let out a moan of agony. Slowly, she raised her head to confront the man who dared touch Faye, let alone threaten her. For a moment, she looked into Faye's face and saw nothing but terror. Ignoring the stab of grief that pierced her at the thought she repulsed Faye, she focused on the stupid man who would die tonight.

"I said, I suggest you let her go," Saxon growled and took a step closer. The knife remained at Faye's throat, keeping Saxon from attacking, but barely.

The man's eyes widened. "Jesus, Mary, and Joseph," he muttered. "You're a fucking vampire."

Saxon smiled. The look was pure evil and showed the length of her fangs. She took another step. "Stop." The man started pulling Faye back with him again, moving faster now, but the knife shook in his hand. Saxon tried to be patient, but in seconds, the stalker would be able to turn the corner around the end of the trailer, and she would lose sight of them.

Running out of time, Saxon clenched her fists and let out another hiss of fury. "No matter where you take her, I will find you," she threatened. "I promise you." Pleased, she watched the horrified man start to lose his grip on Faye. If the knife dropped, he was a dead man. Yet, before the attacker took another step, the last thing Saxon would have imagined happened. Faye fainted. She suddenly collapsed, slipped from the stalker's grasp straight to the ground in a heap.

"Fuck," the stalker yelled and took off at a sprint past the end of the trailer.

Saxon leaped to the spot where he was last standing, only to see him running for his life. With a grin, she was ready to pursue when she realized Faye wasn't moving. She lay there on the ground, blood on her neck, her face pale, and Saxon's mind whirled with possibilities, including a heart attack from fear. Conflicted, Saxon didn't know what to do. Every part of her was filled with hate for the man, but Faye possibly needed her more. With a growl of frustration, she let him go for the moment and moved to Faye's side. She needed to check her pulse, but the blood on Faye's neck continued to overwhelm Saxon's senses. Its presence made her unable to change back to just Saxon.

Then, Faye's eyes started to flutter, and Saxon felt the weight of her own fear lift off her chest. She was alive, but when her eyes opened, and she saw Saxon, terror still filled them. "Please don't kill me," she whispered, and Saxon hated frightening her. Faye meant so much, but the woman's blood was making her crazy.

"I won't," she said as gently as she could, yet it was hard to keep still. "But I need you to go into your trailer and lock the door. Right now."

Her head spinning and heart pounding, Faye rolled away from Saxon and climbed to her feet. Without a look back, she raced up the three metal steps to her trailer door and yanked it open. Trembling, she was inside and bolting the flimsy latch within seconds, but there was no doubt in her mind Saxon could rip the door off the hinges if she wanted. Faye prayed there was enough of the Saxon she cared about in control.

"Did you lock the door?" she heard Saxon growl from the other side. Her voice was close, and Faye guessed the woman was standing on the steps.

"Yes," Faye answered, her whole body shaking. "What else should I do?" There was no answer for a moment, and the waiting made Faye even more anxious. Saxon the vampire could be doing anything. "Are you still there?"

"Call Louis. Not anybody else," she finally said and rattled off the number. "Tell him to come here. He won't hesitate."

Faye swallowed, taking her cellphone from her bag on the trailer's couch. "What will you do?" she asked, not sure she really wanted the answer but afraid not to know.

"I'm going to go get the stalker," she said, and then Faye felt a light sway in the trailer as Saxon left the stairs. Slowly, she let out a long breath, trying to calm her racing heart. This was madness, and a part of her wondered if she was having a nightmare. Saxon being a vampire could not be real, merely a strange side effect influenced by the movie they were making. Yet, as she looked at the phone and punched in Louis' number, the rational part of her believed what was happening was very real.

Thankfully, he answered on the first ring. "What's wrong?" he asked, and Faye wondered how he knew. He couldn't have recognized her private number but then guessed the phone was only used when something bad happened.

"It's Faye," she answered. "Saxon's... she..." With every second that passed, things seemed more and more impossible. She sank down onto the trailer's narrow couch. "She's a..." Faye was having trouble even saying the word.

"Where are you?" Louis asked, his voice all business, and Faye told him the location. She waited while he sounded like he was writing it down.

"Louis," she said, not exactly sure what she was hoping the man would say to the question she was about to ask him, but a part of her still felt a connection to Saxon.

"What is it?" Louis asked, and Faye took a deep breath.

"What can I do to help her?"

There was no hesitation in Louis' response. "Are you bleeding?" he asked, and Faye nodded although he couldn't see her.

"Yes," she whispered.

"Then stay away from her. I'll be there in thirty minutes."

18

S axon followed the man's scent as far as the apartment building's parking lot where they were filming earlier, and then the trail died. Nothing remained but a pair of tire marks where he laid rubber getting away. She'd scared him, but she gave him too much of a head start, and frustration filled her. Somehow, she would find him, and the man would pay. She would never forget his scent.

Hissing in frustration, she stood in the parking lot and forced herself to relax. The aroma of Faye's blood lingered in her senses, but slowly the smell was dissipating. She hoped changing back could happen before she was at Faye's trailer. Louis would be on his way too. Things could still be okay, and she started retracing her steps, eager to talk to Faye through the locked door. She needed to explain things, and she hoped the woman would be in a state of mind to listen. Saxon would be patient, ready to wait until whenever Faye was ready. Tonight, things were likely to be too raw, and she remembered the look of terror in her eyes earlier. Definitely raw.

Before she was back on the path leading to the trailers,

she heard someone coming up behind her. Slowing her steps, hoping the stalker was back, Saxon waited before turning.

"Well, what have we here?" came a man's voice.

A second guy chuckled. "Yeah," he said. "Somebody walking all alone out here at this time of night."

Saxon knew East LA was notorious for gang activity. Trouble from two gangbangers was the last thing she needed right now, and she glanced over her shoulder at the two men. Dressed in LA Laker jerseys and basketball shorts each wore an assortment of gold chains. She had no doubt their many tattoos all had meaning, possibly to show their alliances or accomplishments. Tonight, could be a very bad night for them. "I don't want any trouble," Saxon said, not turning so she didn't draw attention to her changed state. "So, go away."

The men laughed. "Did you hear that?" he said. "She doesn't want trouble." Then, Saxon heard the click of a knife opening. "How about you take off that three-hundred-dollar jacket you're wearing?"

Saxon closed her eyes for a second, gathering herself. She tried to calm enough to change back to her normal state, but the two men were making that impossible. "I warned you," she whispered, more to herself than to them. Then, Saxon whirled around, her eyes blazing and mouth open showing her pointed teeth. "Get away from me if you want to see the sunrise tomorrow." The two men froze, shock on their faces at the horrifying sight. A monster straight from hell stood before them, and when Saxon started toward them, the one with the knife backed away so fast he fell on his ass. The second grabbed his friend by the back of his jersey and started to drag him to his feet.

"Come on," he yelled. "Come on."

As they fled, Saxon hissed at them for good measure but regretted having to show her face. Narrowing her eyes, she considered what the stalker might do with what he saw tonight. It wasn't like he could easily sell his story to a tabloid if he wanted to keep his identity a secret. She wondered if anyone would believe him if he did try. Maybe one of those two-bit rags about two-headed alien babies, but she doubted anyone else would even listen. All she could do was hope not. With a sigh, she turned back to go find Faye and hoped there would be no more trouble tonight.

"Faye?" came the sound of Saxon's voice through the locked trailer door. She was sitting on the couch, rocking back and forth, trying not to entirely freak out over everything that happened. The attack by the stalker, being held at knife-point, Saxon changing into a vampire…

Hearing that Saxon was back made her heart rate jump up a notch, and she heard it pounding her ears. She wondered if Saxon heard the sound too. There was no way to know what kind of powers she had, and that made her even more frightening. Then, an idea struck her. That was the reason she felt so safe around Saxon. Because of the vast power contained within her, but which also changed her into a monster. And yet, Faye wasn't so sure if that was the best way to describe her. As afraid as she was, she also wanted to know more. "Yes, I'm here," she murmured. "Are you still a…?" A part of her didn't want to say the word because then it really would be true and not a dream.

"A vampire?" Saxon replied, and hearing her say it made Faye shiver. "No. I'm me again. But don't open the door, okay?"

Faye swallowed hard, not liking the sound of that request. "Okay," she said. "Why? Are you still dangerous?"

There was a pause, and she wondered if Saxon didn't want to reply. Then, when she thought maybe Saxon had left altogether, the woman answered. "I'm sorry. But yes, a little. Just wait for Louis to come."

Faye nodded, trying to calm herself and stop the rocking. At least Saxon sounded like Saxon again and was being honest with her. Everything was so surreal. Less than an hour ago, she tried to think of the words to convince Saxon to let her come back to her bed. Faye felt such an attraction to her, but now she wasn't sure what she felt. What she needed most were answers. "How long have you been like this?" she asked, wondering if the myths were true that vampires lived forever. Then, she heard a noise on the stairs, and the trailer moved a little. Faye stood and backed away from the door. "What are you doing?"

"Sitting down on the steps," Saxon said. "I didn't mean to scare you. It's easier to talk through the door this way."

Faye let out the breath she was holding and went back to her spot on the couch. She wrapped her arms around herself, trying to reconcile the Saxon on the stairs chatting with her to what she saw tonight. "It's okay. Just stay outside," she said. "Are you going to tell me how long you've been...?" Again, the words stuck in her throat.

"Well over a hundred years," she answered. "A long time to me, but not compared to some."

The word 'some' caught Faye's attention. "How many of you are there?"

"I'm not entirely sure. We don't have hierarchies or an intricate coven like the books and TV imply," she said. "For the most part, we are on our own, trying to fit in." Faye furrowed her brow, surprised because pop culture implied things so differently. "And we are hunted. That part is true."

"Hunted," Faye repeated the word, and for the first time tonight, she felt a little spark of compassion for Saxon the vampire. Replaying the events that happened in her mind, it seemed like Saxon hadn't wanted to change. There was even a cry of pain. "Saxon, do you like being a vampire?" Her voice was just above a whisper. The question was so personal, yet she needed to know.

"No," the woman said without hesitation. "Not anymore."

There was a long silence from inside the trailer, and Saxon guessed Faye was trying to process not only her answer but everything that had happened. There was every reason she would be traumatized, and she was happy Faye didn't appear to have gone into shock. But Faye had a strong character, and Saxon felt proud of her for dealing with everything so well. For a moment, Saxon remembered the first time she saw a vampire. The situation had been so different, so passionate, and in that moment, everything Saxon wanted. Although she hated being a vampire now, she never regretted that night, and a wave of sadness washed over her as she remembered Susan. The woman had been her world, and their love was everything to her.

"Are you all right?" Saxon finally asked, knowing the question was the understatement of the century. Faye was far from all right but going into shock still presented a risk, so she wanted to keep her talking. "I mean, under the circumstances."

"I'm okay," she replied. "Just hoping Louis gets here soon."

Saxon nodded. "Me too. He's a fast driver. It won't take much longer," she said. "Ask me another question."

"Why can't you come near me?" she asked, a quiver in her voice. "You're normal again, right?"

Saxon sighed. She wanted to frame the answer in a way to keep from scaring Faye, but this was a time for honesty too. "Because you're bleeding," she said. "And the aroma makes me crazy."

"Oh," Faye said. "But I think it's stopped."

"I don't want to risk the wound starting again. Louis will have a blood clotting bandage for you," she said, willing the man to arrive soon. The waiting was clearly hard on Faye. As if her thoughts conjured him, the sound of familiar footsteps came from around the trailer. Saxon stood and watched as Louis appeared. He had dressed as if this was any other night with a small black backpack on his shoulder. All that was different was the silver cross the size of a shoebox on a leather strap around his neck. Saxon's whole body stiffened at the sight, and she felt the metal repelling her while making her weak. Wearing the cross was necessary to ensure Louis was protected if Saxon changed again and the thing hurt her eyes to look at it. Plus, the thought he needed it made her sad. He was her closest and dearest friend, yet when she took vampire form, sometimes she was unpredictable.

"Where is she?" he asked without preamble, and as she backed away, Saxon nodded toward the trailer door.

"Inside," she said. "Locked the door, and I've done my best. But I can still smell her blood."

Louis went to the steps, and Saxon backed up further. He didn't have to warn her to stay away. The power of the silver cross was extreme. The thing was also a holy relic and one of the few objects that would repel her. If she touched it, the cross would melt her flesh. "Faye," he called through the door. "I need you to let me in." After a moment, the door opened a crack, and Faye peeked out. When Faye saw Louis, Saxon winced at seeing tears come to her eyes.

"Oh, thank God," she said and threw her arms around Louis' neck as he led her back into the trailer and shut the door. Saxon felt her whole body relax as soon as the cross was out of sight. Unlike most of the silly antics in the movie she was directing, silver and anything truly holy did hurt vampires. Which was why she knew in a few minutes, Faye would come out with Louis wearing a smaller but equally powerful silver cross around her neck. She wouldn't have to wear it forever as Saxon felt her body becoming more and more relaxed by the second. Because of the change in smell, she knew Faye's neck was bandaged with iodine. Louis would take the time to explain the state of things going forward, and if Faye was willing to accept the new situation, everything would be all right. If not, as much as it would hurt, Saxon would leave her be and disappear to start another life in the morning.

19

"Wait," Faye said, her eyes widening with alarm and her hand on the car's passenger door handle. "You're not a vampire, are you?"

Louis shook his gray-haired head as he settled into the driver's seat and put on his seatbelt. "No," he answered, starting the Lexus LC. "I'm Saxon's lifelong assistant, but I'm mortal."

Faye relaxed, but only a little, in the plush leather seat. So far, the night was one terrifying moment after another, and her nerves were beyond on edge. "And that's why you can wear the cross," she said. "And why you were able to put this smaller one around my neck." She looked down at where the intricate piece of jewelry rested on her chest. No longer than her thumb, the cross was elegant with a red gem at the center she guessed was a ruby but reminded her of a drop of blood. Not something she would wear on a day-to-day basis, as it had the look and feel of an heirloom, but gorgeous just the same.

"It's been blessed by a priest as well as dipped in holy water," Louis explained after he noticed she was looking at the cross. "No vampire will come near the necklace. As long as you wear it, Saxon will stay well away, changed or otherwise." Giving the necklace a last look, she tried to decide how she felt about keeping Saxon at bay. The woman left ahead of them with only a sad lingering look at Faye before she went to her car. Faye hadn't known what to think, and a whirlwind of emotions still threatened to overwhelm her any second. She was having trouble reconciling Saxon, her lover, and Saxon the vampire.

"But you're not wearing your cross anymore?" Faye said, having noticed he put his in the trunk before getting into the car.

Louis started out of the parking lot. He looked tired. "No," he said. "Saxon won't hurt me, especially considering she is back in her normal state. She probably wouldn't have earlier, but I wore the cross as a safety precaution. Your phone call was alarming." His face grew somber. "But I suggest you keep yours on until we figure out the plan for tonight. Which makes me ask, is there someplace specific you want to go? I can stay with you at a hotel until we arrange security or some other setup. Unless you would prefer something else?"

Faye furrowed her brow. Considering the night's events and her reactions so far, there was no wonder Louis asked about options. Still, she thought they would go to Saxon's home all along but then realized Louis didn't want to presume. There were obvious reasons why she might not feel comfortable. Strangely, even after all that happened, she did want Saxon. Just as before, there was no doubt in her mind the woman would protect her from any threat. It seemed especially true tonight, knowing the information that she did. A random thought crossed her mind that there seemed no better defense than having a vampire on watch.

Assuming she remained safe from the vampire herself. "If you think Saxon can contain herself, then I want to go to her house," Faye said, and Louis gave her a smile of reassurance.

"With your bleeding stopped and the cut well bandaged, she will act normal. The same as she did before tonight," Louis explained. "It is the sight and smell of blood that she struggles with, especially yours."

Thinking about what he said, she realized their undeniable chemistry was possibly why her blood was incredibly potent and therefore dangerous. Strangely, she didn't know what to think about that fact. His words confirmed what until a few hours ago she hoped to be true—that Saxon genuinely wanted her. The charade about Saxon taking advantage of her and thus making their relationship professional all stemmed from her need to hide she was a vampire. "Would she ever have told me on her own?" Faye whispered as Louis took the onramp to the freeway.

He looked thoughtful while he maneuvered to get them into the fast lane. "I think so," he finally said, glancing over. "She cares for you a great deal. I've not seen her like this for a very long time."

Faye let what he said sink in. "I've never felt like this about anyone either," she confessed, listening to her emotions while trying to hold back her fear from tonight. "We've only known each other for a few weeks, but I am drawn to her. She's all I think about, and even though I now know her secret, I believe I feel the same." She shook her head, amazing even herself that she felt so open to this new reality. "Does that make me sound crazy?"

"A little," Louis said, but he was smiling. "When we get to her house, I'll text to let her know she can come home."

Raising her eyebrows, Faye hadn't considered Saxon would stay away from her own house. "Thank you," she said. "I don't want her to have to hide from me. In fact, I want to know more about her."

"Then, it sounds like the two of you have a lot to talk about," Louis said, relief clear in his voice as he took the exit that would lead them to the freeeway to Malibu.

Saxon felt the phone buzz in her lap and knew it was a text from Louis. Parked only a couple miles from her home, at one of the gravel pullouts along the Pacific Coast Highway, she had been waiting to hear from him. Trying to be patient, every nerve in her body was on edge. This would be a message about Faye and her state of mind. All Saxon could do was hope the woman was all right, no matter her decisions.

Unable to stand it any longer, she read the words. "She's okay. With me at the house. You can come home." Saxon felt the weight of all her worst fears lift off her chest. Faye must not think she was a monster if she was willing to stay at her house. Still, it was too much to hope the woman felt any desire toward her, not after tonight. All she wished is they would remain friends, maybe even enough to finish the movie. Saxon would take any chance to stay near her a little longer.

"I'll be there in a minute," she wrote back and pulled onto the highway. Louis was waiting outside when she parked. His presence did not feel promising, and as Saxon climbed out of the car, she hoped Faye hadn't changed her mind. "What's wrong? Did she leave?"

Louis held out his hands to calm Saxon. "Nothing like that," he said. "But I wanted to warn you that she is badly shaken over this, yet openminded." He smiled. "You have a special woman in this one. Tread lightly so you don't frighten her away."

"Thank you, Louis," Saxon said with a nod. "Once again, you have been there for me."

Louis gave a short bow. "That is my role," he said and followed behind her as Saxon walked into her house. Expecting every light in the place to be on to reassure Faye, only the two lamps on the end tables were lit. When she looked across the great room and out through the giant sliding glass doors which made up the entire ocean-facing wall, Faye's silhouette showed she was on the balcony. Again, Saxon was surprised. That seemed a vulnerable space with no place to hide.

Glancing at Louis, she saw he looked a little surprised too. "What did she say to you?" Saxon asked. "In the car."

"Not much, actually," he replied. "She was thoughtful and quiet most of the way. A few questions, but I said she needed to talk to you. After all, it is your story to tell. She is still wearing the necklace with the cross pendant, though. So be mindful of it."

"I understand," Saxon said, walking across the room until she was at the door.

Calming her nerves for a moment, she tried to contain her expectations about Faye's response. The fact she was there at all was a miracle. Then, she slid open the door enough to step through. Faye, standing at the railing, turned. A glint of moonlight reflected off the silver cross. Saxon froze. Although, because it was smaller, the thing did not have the power of the one Louis wore earlier, seeing it made her muscles tense. Still, she held her ground. Talking to Faye was worth any discomfort. "I'm sorry," she said, not sure how else to start the conversation. The night was one neither would ever forget. There seemed no words to say to apologize for what happened.

Faye crossed her arms, regarding Saxon for a moment, as if not sure she accepted the apology. "You scared the hell out of me tonight," she finally said. "I thought I might die."

All Saxon did was nod. The woman had been so afraid at one point that she fainted. "I know," Saxon said. "I never meant for this to happen."

In the moonlight, Faye looked at Saxon's face and saw nothing but sadness and remorse. She had no doubt every word she was saying was true. Yet, things did happen, and Faye was still not sure how to process them. "Would you have ever told me?" she asked, repeating the same question she asked Louis but still needing an answer directly from Saxon. Although, a part of her wondered a little what she would have done if she had known. "And is this the real reason you wanted to back away from our relationship?"

Saxon looked away, over the rail at the ocean while Faye waited. "Maybe," she said at last. Then, she turned back to gaze into Faye's eyes. The mesmerizing power, the pull, was still there, and Faye felt it all through her body. No matter what happened, a part of her still craved the woman's touch. "Probably. You're special to me. More than I can express with words."

Not sure what to think, Faye bit her lip and tried to keep from turning to mush at Saxon's words. Her feelings were the same, and as they stood face to face with the sound of the ocean waves behind them, everything felt normal. Not thinking, she touched the cross hanging against her chest and watched Saxon flinch. Seeing her reaction brought everything back into focus. Saxon Montague was a vampire. With scarlet eyes and fangs. There was no way around the fact, and she didn't know what she was going to do. Nothing in her life prepared her for this situation. Yet, she knew Saxon was important to her, and she wasn't ready to walk away. Holding Saxon's gaze, Faye reached up and unclasped the silver chain around her neck. She saw the woman's eyes widen, and her body was shaking. "If this is going to work," Faye said, turning to hold the cross above the table furthest from where they were standing. "I have to be able to trust you. Can I?"

Saxon's eyes darted from the cross and then back to Faye's face. "Yes," she replied. "I promise on my existence."

Faye dropped the chain to the glass tabletop and walked toward Saxon. She watched her visibly relax, and hope filled her eyes. "Then, let's go inside," she said. "And talk. I want to know everything."

20

NEW YORK CITY, 1926

"Darling, you look adorable," Susan said as she pushed a short lock of Saxon's dark-brown hair back into place. "I don't know why we didn't cut it years ago." Saxon grinned. She liked the new hairstyle a lot and ran her hand along the slicked back side before putting on her fedora. When her hair wasn't swathed in Brilliantine, it covered her ears, but tonight she looked quite dapper in the backseat of the yellow cab rattling along 54th street.

Saxon leaned over and pecked Susan's rouge colored cheek. "Thank you, sweetheart," she said. "I want to look good for you."

With a smile, Susan took her hand and gave it a squeeze. "You always do," she said, a twinkle in her eye. "And I'm so excited about tonight." So was Saxon. They were spending the evening in one of New York's most popular speakeasies —the 300 Club. It was something they looked forward to every Friday night since returning from Paris six months before. Although Saxon had enjoyed their latest tour of Europe, she preferred to be back in the big cities of the United States. Everything was so exciting with endless possibilities. A nation growing so fast, it boggled the mind. Reading the newspaper every morning, there seemed to be a new invention announced daily. No place was like America.

Saxon watched out the window as the cab pulled up to wait in the line of taxis dropping off people eager to get inside. It was an unusually warm autumn night, and everyone had dressed to the nines. Some men were in suits with white, black, even checkered jackets, while others wore button-down dress shirts with suspenders holding up loose fitting pants. All wore hats of some type or another, and she saw a lot of wingtip shoes, just like her own, but what was most spectacular were the women.

If there was anything Saxon liked most about this decade, it was the way the women dressed. Hemlines so short some people called them scandalous. Silk, beads, and rhinestones made them shimmer in an array of daring colors. Susan, beside her, looked incredibly sensational tonight. In her midnight blue sequined flapper dress, ruffle white turban hat, and matching chiffon stole, few compared to her class and charm.

When they reached the front of the building, Saxon jumped out to hold the door for Susan as she slid across the seat. Laughter and music spilled out the front doors of the club, and Saxon was already tapping her foot to the beat. She loved to dance, and the two of them would practice all night long to each new trend in their living room as jazz played on the Victrola. Then, on Fridays they would show off their new moves, much to the pleasure of the other dancers who often stood back to watch the show. There was no time and no place Saxon felt happier than there with Susan in New York. As Susan took her arm, Saxon gave her a smile. "Ready?" she asked, and Susan smiled back with the same love she felt reflected in her dark eyes.

"Always," she said, and they strode into the club where the atmosphere was electric. Crowds of people intermixed with celebrities, entertainers, and of course, the club's famous fan dancers packed the place. The only spot not constantly overrun by partygoers was the dancefloor and the small stage where the band played. Even then, it wasn't unusual for an intoxicated patron to crash into couples doing the Charleston. Still, the night was all in good fun, and no one took offense. As Saxon and Susan made their way through the crowd, acquaintances said hello or gave them a nod. They had no real friends, and that was by choice. Getting close to people only added complications if they decided to disappear from their current life to start a new one.

Saxon watched as Susan scanned the crowd, and she knew the woman was looking for a fresh face. Someone who hadn't been there before and looked out of place or overwhelmed. These were the ones new to New York, fresh from the Nebraska cornfields or something similar. After a moment, Susan smiled and leaned close to speak in Saxon's ear to be heard over the music.

"How about the little blonde to the left of the stage? The one with the wide eyes who keeps biting her lip?" she asked, and Saxon followed her gaze. The girl looked young and indeed out of her league. A slightly older girl was beside her, who seemed a little less stunned by the speakeasy's madness, and Saxon guessed they were cousins or something similar. That one might have come to New York a year before the other and professed to be an expert on the ins and outs of the city's nightlife.

"I see her," she replied. "But she's not alone."

Susan squeezed her arm. "It will still work," she said. "Consider it a special treat. Let's join them, but first, order us a round of drinks, will you, darling?" Without waiting for an answer, the woman made her way through the crowd toward the girls. Saxon watched her go and appreciated the form she cut as people parted to let her through. The two newcomers didn't stand a chance. Susan was incredibly mesmerizing tonight. If this Friday went like the others, the four of them would be out on the dancefloor before long. They would all be enjoying the night, and the unsuspecting girls would be having the time of their lives. After all, this was why they came to the big city in the first place.

Turning away, Saxon examined the two-person-deep crowd at the bar. Of course, no one was legitimately buying alcohol, but the coffee had a hell of a punch. It was going to take some maneuvering to get what she needed, but before she hardly made progress, someone pressed up beside her. His presence made Saxon's skin crawl, and she reared back, looking to see what the stranger was doing. What she saw made her grimace. A man in a black fedora, dressed in a double-breasted black suit, stood looking at her and he wore a silver cross around his neck. With a sudden grin that had no humor in it, he took a step closer. "I'm sorry," he said. "Did I startle you?" Saxon pushed into the back of the man behind her, making him curse, but she needed space. Every muscle in her body quivered and it was more than the cross. Something wasn't right.

"Get away from me," Saxon hissed and felt an unfamiliar fury starting to rise. If she didn't get away soon, Saxon worried she might not be able to keep from changing.

With a little laugh, the stranger stepped closer, and just as Saxon thought she couldn't hold back any longer, a man came running in the front door. "The Feds are here," he yelled in a panic. In an instant, the club became a madhouse.

Using the chaos to her advantage, Saxon started elbowing her way through the throng. Her only thought was getting to Susan. The man with the cross upset her badly, and she needed to find Susan before he did. Then they would make their way out one of the speakeasy's many backdoor exits. This was not the first raid they dealt with because the club was a well-known target, but tonight the place was overly crowded. "Susan," she yelled over the other screams and curses. Out of the corner of her eye, she saw the first wave of federal agents burst through the front doors a moment before Susan appeared out of the crowd. Pushing others aside with ease, the woman grabbed Saxon's hand.

"The hidden door under the stairs," she said, her voice calm. "To the blind alley like last time." Saxon didn't resist, and with a last look over her shoulder to ensure they weren't being pursued by the stranger in black, she followed Susan. The two darted past others to make their way to the exit. Soon, they were out in the warm night air, running hand in hand. A few others from the speakeasy were ahead of them, and they followed, knowing where the alley poured onto the street. Luckily, the police never bothered to try and arrest anyone coming out. With everyone smart enough to ditch any booze as they went, and no way to prove for sure they were in the speakeasy, arrests never held up. Besides, being in the club wasn't necessarily a crime. Only caught in possession of alcohol got a person arrested.

As they reached the sidewalk, Saxon slowed them. "Susan, there was someone weird in there," she said, noticing a tremble in her voice. She couldn't seem to shake the way the man upset her, and Susan stopped.

Looking into Saxon's face, as if trying to read her thoughts, she put a hand on her cheek. "What happened?"

Taking Susan's hand, Saxon tried to put into words how it felt but couldn't quite decide why he was so frightening. "I was waiting to order us drinks, and then there was this man beside me," she said. "In a black suit, fancy so he fit in, but maybe like he didn't always dress that way." Saxon swallowed hard. "And he was wearing a silver cross."

Susan narrowed her eyes. "Did he say anything?" she asked, and Saxon tried hard to remember.

"I think he apologized for bumping into me," she said. "But I'm not sure. He was making me upset, angry, and I was afraid I would change."

After a long look over Saxon's shoulder into the dark alley, Susan started them walking again. "Of course, you were upset, darling," she said, her voice light as if nothing concerned her. "But I'm sure the man was nothing more than a devote Christian." Saxon opened her mouth to explain it felt like he was more than that, but before she did, Susan flashed her a smile. "Please, let's not let him ruin our evening. Now hail us a cab and take me to Central Park. I'm still hungry."

21

Thankful for the cloudy, rainy day, Saxon had set up her position under one of the many canopies in place at the edge of their filming location. It was not that she enjoyed dealing with trying to keep everything dry. Bad weather hampered filming and meant they were moving at a snail's pace this afternoon. Still, the thick midday cloud cover kept her from being uncomfortable. Direct sunlight wasn't deadly but gave her a wicked sunburn, so she'd convinced the writers to move the outdoor scene to a rainy day for extra effect. Finally, the weather cooperated with Saxon, and the old, unkempt cemetery was proving to be dismal indeed.

Unfortunately, Faye was struggling too, and Saxon blamed herself. For three days, the woman stayed at her home but slept in the guest room. Even after Saxon answered most of her questions, Faye kept her at arm's length. She could tell the physical attraction remained, but not the same trust. Saxon understood but losing Faye still hurt. Tonight, though, the awkward situation could be solved. Word had come that Faye's estate was ready for her to move back in. She had the whole place sanitized, and the walls repainted. To make sure no trace of the man remained, she even replaced some of her furniture. She also installed a new security system, with help available around the clock. Yet, Saxon didn't like the fact she and Faye would be separated, and after filming today, she hoped they could talk more about her safety.

At least the other actor with Faye, playing a fellow FBI agent, was a good sport under the difficult circumstances. As much as Saxon tried to catch what she wanted in one or two takes, the slippery ground and gusting wind made things challenging. "Action," Saxon shouted to try again. The scene involved Agent Kolchak and her new, unwelcome partner walking among the headstones. They were searching each trying to find a specific family name. Many of them were partially covered with weeds, thanks to mother nature and a little help from the special effects crew, requiring Faye to push aside the overgrowth to see the names. All of which was filmed by the second camera operator who walked with them. Within all those variables, Saxon struggled to get what she wanted. Crossing her fingers, she hoped this was the one.

Watching through the viewer in front of her, she saw exactly what the second cameraman filmed. Faye finally reached the first of a group of headstones with the surname she was looking for chiseled in them. Her eyes widened slightly as she pulled back a tall fern. Satisfaction was on her face. "Cut," Saxon said, and all eyes turned to her, wanting to know if she got the shot she was looking for, and she nodded. "I like it. Let's move on." With a huge group sigh of relief, the crew began to prepare for the next scene. From her chair, Saxon watched Faye slog across the wet ground to her tent. A production assistant was already at the door with a towel in her hand. Drying off would require added time with hair and makeup before shooting again to ensure she looked the same for the next series of takes. Still, Saxon would not ask her to stay drenched and uncomfortable. By now, Faye was most likely half undressed and wrapped in a blanket. Saxon tried not to think about how the wet clothing clinging to her body might look and instead checked her phone.

For the last three days, Saxon skimmed the Hollywood Reporter and other entertainment websites. She looked for any mention of vampires. There were minor references to the filming of *Venandi* but nothing else. Next, she scrolled through social media and again—still nothing. Not surprised, she figured reporters would ignore claims of anyone turning into a creature of the night. Even if the stalker made it past the front desk to talk to someone, people would think he simply saw someone in costume. Still, the episode upset her on too many levels and was even more reason she needed to talk privately to Faye. The stalker was still dangerous and knew Saxon was a vampire.

Shivering, Faye felt cold and miserable sitting in her chair, wrapped in the warm fleece blanket they had ready for her. Matters weren't helped by the fact her acting sucked today. No one needed to tell her directly, because she had enough experience in the business to feel when she was off. The problem was not forgetting her lines but staying in character was a struggle. She knew why and that frustrated her even more. Saxon Montague. Today Faye needed to make a decision, not just for her safety, but for her heart.

With the news she could move back into her house in Beverly Hills, she didn't know what to do. Since learning

Saxon's secret, their relationship changed dramatically. Finding out about her past and how she first became a vampire had shaken Faye. It made what she could have chalked up to a nightmare a reality. On top of that, her stalker was still out there somewhere, no doubt even more intrigued. Although there was no message from him since the attack, Faye didn't think he had given up. His motivation was clear—he wanted Faye for himself.

After talking to Saxon at length about what happened the other night by her trailer, she did not go to the police. Aside from possibly complicating things for Saxon, the attacker wore a ski mask, and she hadn't recognized his voice. There really wasn't much to report, which made her feel vulnerable and afraid. Unless she was with Saxon. Even knowing as much as she did about the woman, Faye felt safe when she was with her. Louis' words in the car as they drove to Saxon's house, that Saxon cared very much for her, kept coming to mind. Right now, she was giving Faye space, and she appreciated it, but tonight something had to change. Either she would choose to trust Saxon entirely again, or she would go home and hope with the new security her stalker couldn't get to her.

There was a knock at the door of the tent. "Is it all right if I come in?" she heard Saxon ask, obviously making sure Faye was decent. Not that she hadn't seen all of Faye, but this was different, and she appreciated her consideration.

"Come in," Faye said and then looked at her production assistant. "Would you go get me some extra hot coffee, please?"

The girl nodded as Saxon stepped in. "Absolutely," the assistant said. "Is there anything else you need?"

Faye smiled. "That's all for right now. And take your time. I want to talk to Ms. Montague."

The production assistant darted out, leaving Saxon and Faye alone. She looked into the woman's eyes and felt the familiar flutter of butterflies when she saw the desire there. "How are you holding up?" Saxon said, clearly trying to keep things light and professional. "I know this rain is making everything harder."

Faye held the gaze but tried to take a similar professional approach. "I'm not helping," she said. "My acting is lousy today."

For a moment, Saxon didn't say anything as she continued to look in her eyes. The pull to touch her was intense. The look on the woman's face told her the same, and she had the strongest desire to hold out her hand for Saxon to take. Being held by her would feel so wonderful. So reassuring. Still, she held back, not sure if she was ready, and Saxon dropped her eyes to look at her hands. "You have good reasons to be struggling today," she said. "Which is why I am here."

"I'm not sure what I'm going to do yet," Faye said with a shake of her head. "I can't keep hiding. I have a life." Then, she paused, not sure if she wanted to say the next few words but knowing the time had come to decide. Tears threatened, but she fought to hold back any more emotion. Facts were facts. Saxon was a vampire who could be dangerous at times, even toward her. "And staying with you is too hard. I feel things that confuse me, and this can't go on forever."

"Things that confuse you," Saxon repeated, more to herself than to Faye. "I see." Not wanting Faye to see the pain on her face, she turned to leave. There was nothing more to say.

Faye stood up from her chair. "Wait," she said, and

Saxon hesitated. "Please understand. I don't mean to hurt you, but I don't know what to do about how I feel."

Saxon fought to keep all emotion out of her voice. "I understand," she said. "Do you still want a ride to your house after filming ends today?"

At the question, Faye moved closer and then touched her arm. Unable to help her reaction, she stiffened at the contact. There was no way she could keep her body from responding to Faye, no matter what the woman said to her. "Saxon," she whispered. "Please don't think I've stopped wanting you. I just don't think I can." Conflicted, Saxon didn't move although they were only inches apart. The heat coming from the blanket around Faye warmed Saxon and only made Faye more desirable. Looking at Faye's mouth, the actress was biting her lip, and Saxon knew a part of her wanted to be kissed. She just didn't know if Faye realized it or not. Incapable of stopping and knowing this might be the last time, Saxon gently kissed her. Faye hesitated for only a second before returning the embrace, and passion flared between them.

Slipping her hands under the blanket and around Faye's waist, Saxon realized she was in only a bra and panties. Faye moaned at the contact, and Saxon pulled her closer. All the wanting from the last few days was pent up inside her and, taking the kiss deeper, Saxon let her desire take over. As much as Faye said they couldn't be together, everything else about her sent a different message. Wanting more, Saxon broke the kiss and ran her lips along her neck, feeling the woman's heart beat faster. Faye was so alive, and Saxon felt the familiar tug inside her, but she buried it deep as she pushed the blanket off her shoulder.

"Wait," Faye gasped against Saxon's cheek. "You're making me crazy." She put her hands on Saxon's chest and gently pushed. "And this is exactly why I can't be around you."

Closing her eyes in frustration but respecting what Faye said, Saxon stepped away. Still, in her mind, their story wasn't over. "Let me take you home tonight," she said, and when Faye opened her mouth to answer, she held up a hand to stop her so she could finish. "I just want to make sure everything is safe."

Saxon watched Faye search her face as if there were answers to everything there, but then she went to sit back in her chair. "Yes. Thank you," she said without meeting Saxon's eyes. "I want that too."

22

"And here is the second panic button," the head of the private security team said, pointing at a red push button on the wall. Big, burly, with a flak jacket and handgun, he looked every part the role of protection. Faye felt confident he knew his job, yet a hint of fear at being home alone still lingered. The sensation of her private space being violated would not go away.

"Thank you," she said, looking at the red button beside her bed. Its twin was in the kitchen. They were strategically placed where she spent a large majority of her time, but she prayed she would never use them.

With Saxon behind her, Faye trailed after the security guard as he led them back into the main living room. "And I think that covers it," he said as they finished his tour, explaining what was in place for her safety. "Any questions?"

"No," Faye said. "At least not at the moment. Thank you."

"Just doing my job," he said with a smile, walking to the front door. "And don't hesitate to use those buttons. We will be here in minutes." Faye nodded as the security guard left. She turned the three locks behind him before putting her forehead against the door. Everything seemed overwhelming, and as much as she wanted it to, her house did not feel like her home anymore. "Hey," Saxon said, her voice gentle and a touch concerned. "Come sit down and let yourself relax for a minute. I'll get you a glass of water."

"Screw water," Fays said, stepping away from the door and looking at Saxon. "I want wine. A lot of it." Wisely not saying a word, Saxon followed her into the kitchen where she snagged a bottle of pinot gris from the wine fridge and a glass from the shelf. In seconds, the electric opener had the cork out, and she was pouring. herself some. She took a long swallow and sighed, relishing the taste of something cool and light on her tongue. Suddenly, the idea of getting a little drunk appealed to her. If she was going to stay here alone, she would need some liquid courage. Glancing over, she noticed Saxon still watching her over the island. "That was rude, wasn't it?" Grabbing another glass, she set it on the quartz.

"Don't bother," Saxon said with a wave at the second glass. "I don't want any tonight." Faye narrowed her eyes at the answer, wondering for a second at the woman's agenda, but finished her own glass. A warm glow was forming in her empty stomach already. Craft services on location today didn't have anything appealing to her, so she stuck with just coffee and skipped eating. It was not a smart combination, but she didn't care. The big security guard promised her she was safe. And then there was always Saxon.

"Oh, that's right," she said, after another drink. "You can't get intoxicated, so what's the point?"

Saxon tilted her head. "Something like that," she replied, her tone a shade cooler than before, and Faye saw her look at her new glass of wine. It was already half gone. "Let me make us something to eat."

Defiant, Faye finished the glass. "You cook too?" she asked, somehow not surprised. Saxon seemed able to do anything.

She nodded. "I took a few classes," she said. "Over the years." Before Faye replied, Saxon went to the sub-zero refrigerator and opened the doors. After a moment, she glanced back at Faye, who knew the shelves were bare of fresh ingredients since she never had much on hand while filming. "French omelet?"

Faye waved her empty glass, loving the lightheaded feeling the wine gave her. "Over the years," she repeated to Saxon, knowing she was starting to sound a bit confrontational. Still, there were many pent-up frustrations inside her, and after everything, she couldn't take it anymore.

Taking a moment, Saxon kept her eyes on the inside of the refrigerator as she ran through her options on how to handle Faye. Obviously, she was set on getting intoxicated this evening and probably ready to get a few things she'd been holding back out in the open. Thinking there seemed no better time than this evening, Saxon closed the door and went to sit on a stool at the island. "Yes, over the years," she said, keeping her tone neutral and a matter of fact. "I've worked in the restaurant business in a few cities at different points. It's a career I enjoy and look forward to going back to at some point."

Faye snorted a laugh, and Saxon realized she was already tipsier than she thought. Still, she just watched as she took out another bottle of white wine. "You're really something, you know that?" Faye said, working the cork puller. "Young and never age, great body, super strong, sexy as hell." Grabbing her glass, she filled it. "And you're a vampire."

"Well, I don't know about all of it, but yes," Saxon said. "I am a vampire."

"Incredible," Faye said, suddenly with tears in her eyes and the wine bottle in her hand apparently forgotten. "I've fallen hard for you. Do you know that? All I want to do is be close to you, but..."

Saxon moved around the table and caught the wine bottle before Faye dropped it. Setting the thing on the counter beside the wine glasses, Saxon pulled a crying Faye into her arms. "I feel it too," she whispered into the woman's hair. "If you really want to work on us, we can try to find a way."

Faye answered by lifting her face and the tears staining her cheeks made Saxon feel a stab of sadness in her chest. This was not what she wanted. The last thing she ever sought when she came to Los Angeles was to find love, but there was something rare about Faye. There was an undeniable connection that both were fighting but were losing.

"Kiss me," Faye murmured, and for a moment, Saxon wasn't sure. Somehow, she knew if they kissed there in the kitchen, it would be impossible to stop. Her passion for Faye was so strong. Yet, when a look of doubt started to seep into Faye's eyes at Saxon's hesitation, she couldn't stand letting her think even for a second she wasn't all she desired.

Bringing their mouths together, Saxon felt the electricity leap between them. Once again, the heat made Saxon dizzy with want, and when the woman opened her lips to let their tongues collide, she moaned from deep within her. The amount of passion Faye evoked made Saxon crazy. Only Susan had made her tremble with just a kiss, until Faye. Other than Susan, there had never been anyone in her life like this. The feelings Saxon had holding this woman in her arms were buried so long ago she'd forgotten how perfect it felt.

Only by using every ounce of her willpower was Saxon able to break the kiss. Looking into Faye's face, the woman's eyes were closed, and her lips were slightly parted. Her body leaned almost limp against Saxon. "Faye," Saxon said. "Look at me."

Faye opened her eyes, and the gaze held all the emotion Saxon felt. "I don't care," Faye whispered. "I don't want to be without you."

Unable to hold back, Saxon lifted Faye in her arms and carried her to the bedroom.

As they entered the room, Faye reveled in the power she felt coming from Saxon, but this time it frightened her too. Saxon had explained to her the intensity of sex could be too much to hold back a change. If the woman was even half as turned on as Faye, there could be a problem. When Saxon started to lay her back on the bed, Faye resisted. "No," she said, and Saxon stopped, still holding her in her arms.

"What's wrong?" Saxon asked, confusion on her face. "Did I hurt you?"

Faye touched her face and caressed her cheek. "You didn't hurt me," she answered, taking a deep breath before she continued. "But I need to be in charge tonight. If this is going to work."

Faye saw Saxon's eyes widen with surprise, but then a look of anticipation crossed her face. "Okay," she said, setting Faye on her feet. "What do you want me to do?"

Knowing she needed distance, Faye moved to sit in the green wingback chair in the corner of her bedroom. She gave Saxon a sultry smile, liking her decision already. "Take off your shirt," she said, leaning back as she watched the woman slowly and sexily pulled her sweater over her head. Seeing she was naked underneath, Faye sucked in a breath at Saxon's physique. The muscles Saxon earned working the tobacco farm so long ago remained as if frozen in time. Licking her lips, Faye kept going. "Now your belt." Not hesitating, Saxon unhooked the buckle and pulled the leather through her belt loops before dropping it to the floor. The simple move made Faye moan it was so sexy.

Saxon smiled. "Are you okay?" she asked, and Faye raised an eyebrow.

"Did I say you can talk?" she asked. "Shoes and socks." Saxon did, not saying a word, and Faye paused, touching her forefinger to her lips before finishing her requests. Her breath coming quick, she was entirely aroused as an ache built between her legs. "Pants, and whatever is underneath them." Saxon obeyed until she stood naked in front of Faye. Letting her eyes roam the woman's body, her skin was smooth and pale in the bit of light coming through the door from the living room. "You're amazing," was all she could think to say.

Saxon smiled but didn't speak, and the submission brought Faye back to focus. If she was going to tame her vampire, she first needed to take the edge off their lovemaking. "Good," she said and motioned to the bed. "Lie down on your back." Obeying, Saxon did, but Faye stayed in the chair, needing the space to see if her plan would work. Filled with anticipation, she moved to the edge of her seat. "Now, touch yourself. I want to watch you make yourself come."

With no movement at first, Faye thought Saxon might not do what she wanted. Then as she watched, Saxon slid her hands down her body. Slowly, she started to work her fingertips over her center, and Faye felt her own body tighten in response. When Saxon widened her legs a little and moved faster, circling her own clit, it took all of Faye's willpower to stay in the chair. Her need to touch Saxon grew every second. "Keep going," Faye gasped and let out a moan when Saxon arched her back, starting to buck against her own hand.

Her body clearly on edge, Faye watched Saxon's eyes widen and prepared to flee but she waited. "I'm going to come," Saxon growled, and Faye held her breath. If it was going to happen, the time would be now. With a moan, Saxon let go, and her whole body shook with pleasure, but through it all, the woman didn't change.

Watching Saxon's body relax, Faye stood and moved to the bed. "Thank you," she said as she reached for the buttons of her own blouse. "For doing that for me."

"Always," Saxon said, with conviction in her voice. "I would do anything to keep you safe." Faye knew in her heart she meant it.

23

W alking across the quad at the center of the university campus, Saxon contemplated how best to film the next sequence. An unsuspecting coed was being hunted by the vampire, but not to kill like the others. He planned to kidnap her to hold in his basement because Faye's character was getting too close. Not being in this evening's scenes, Faye was back at home until later tonight. When Saxon finished filming, she would pick her up to take her back to the house in Malibu. Two weeks had passed since the night Faye moved back into her house, and they had come a long way, spending time at both homes. Everything had been magical, and thinking of Faye, Saxon felt a longing to be back with her. Their chemistry remained intense and the connection only grew stronger each day.

But first, she had to shoot these scenes. The filming of *Venandi* was close to completion, and Saxon would be glad when it wrapped. Then, she could focus on Faye and figure out what happened next with their relationship. But that was later and trying to refocus, she saw movement in the shadows to her left. Her first assistant director was walking toward her, and he didn't look happy. Hoping this was not about a delay, Saxon waited to hear whatever bad news he was about to give her. For a moment, her mind went to Faye and her stomach clenched. "What's wrong?" Saxon asked, ready to bolt from the set if the woman needed her.

"It's Brad Norris," he said, shaking his head while stopping in front of her. "He is insisting we change the script."

Saxon worked to control her temper. The man was a pain in her ass from the start, and being they were less than a week from wrapping, his request was not going to happen. Somehow, she would have to appease him enough he wouldn't walk off the project in protest. "What does he want?" she asked, then waved her hand to end the conversation. "Never mind, I'll go see him."

Without another word, she walked to the nearby resource center where they set up the actors and crew for tonight's shoot. Brad was easy to find, currently leaning against the wall, chatting with the cute, blonde assistant art director. Saxon shook her head. The man did not stop, always flirting with the nearest willing female. When he saw Saxon approaching, his smile disappeared as he stood up straight. The art director wisely slipped away. "I figured you would show up eventually," Brad said, his charm long gone. "Although it took you long enough."

Saxon worked hard to keep any frustration off her face. Getting into an argument would solve nothing. Still, she couldn't resist a dig. "You looked entertained enough," she said, then got down to business. "Rumor is you're unhappy with the scene."

"Not this scene," Brad corrected. "This one makes me look good."

"Because you're the center of attention," Saxon said

making an observation rather than asking him. "Instead of Faye."

At least the actor blushed a little at his vanity, but then he frowned. "You two are really chummy," he said. "And I think my role is being minimized." The fact wasn't true. The script was never changed to favor either of the actors, but Saxon let him finish. "So, I want a different ending."

Unable to keep the surprise off her face, Saxon tried to imagine what they could possibly revise to favor Brad. Agent Kolchak would use fire to destroy the vampire and save the girl before Brad could turn her into another vampire. The audience would expect no less. "What did you have in mind?" she asked, holding her temper in check. Knowing Brad was a weak human being made it hard for her to stay patient.

Clearly not sensing the danger of upsetting his movie director, a grin spread across his face, and Saxon knew she wasn't going to like his answer. "I get away," he said, clapping his hands together. "They can save the girl, that's fine, but I escape."

"You escape?" Saxon repeated, trying to see the point. The movie was dark, sinister, hopefully frightening, but the vampire hunter had to win.

Brad's eye shone with excitement. "Yes, I escape," he said. "For the sequel."

Sitting in the Polo Lounge at the Beverly Hills Hotel, Faye waited for her best friend Jane to join her for dinner. They needed to catch up. Since the stalker's attack, all they had done was talk on the phone or text. Faye simply could not risk putting her friend and her family in danger. As more time passed though, and not even a whisper from the stalker, she started to relax. Perhaps seeing such a frightening scene that night deterred him from trying anything again. She could understand. Seeing Saxon as a vampire scared her half to death. So far, there was no hint of Saxon's other self, even when their sex was at its most intense and Faye felt more and more confident they would be okay.

Jane waved as she came into the dining room, and after a quick check-in with the maître d, made her way to Faye. Leaning over the table, she gave her friend a kiss on the cheek. "It's so good to see you," Jane said. "I've been so worried."

Faye smiled as her friend sat down. Taking Jane's hand, Faye gave it a squeeze. "Don't be," she said. "I'm okay. I have the best security possible and it's been weeks since anything happened." She leaned back and picked up the drink menu to study it. "And I have Saxon to protect me, of course."

"Ohhh, yes," Jane said, plucking the drink menu out of her hands so she couldn't hide. "I want to know all about that too."

Faye laughed. "I don't even know where to begin," she said. "She's...well... indescribable." The explanation sounded corny, but there really wasn't an easy way to describe Saxon without revealing Saxon's secret. "I've never met anyone like her."

"Okay, I get it," Jane said. "You're head over heels for this woman. I'm guessing you're spending all your time together? On and off set?" A warm feeling came over Faye as she thought about just how much time they did spend together. Trying to maintain a professional distance while filming, but all over each other once they were in the car headed home. The fact they weren't in the news yet was a little surprising, but since the attack, Saxon insisted on a closed set with the utmost security. No one had access to her, and that included reporters or curious fans. Suddenly, Jane was snapping her fingers. "Hello? Earth to Faye?"

Faye blinked, lost in thoughts of her fantastic relationship with Saxon. "Sorry," she said and felt a blush creep up her cheeks. "She just makes me crazy. What did you ask?"

Jane shook her head, but she was grinning ear to ear. "You kind of answered me already," she said and then caught Faye's eye. "I love seeing you like this, but have you thought about what happens once the movie is over?"

"I've been thinking about that," Faye answered. "And I'm going to take some time away from acting. Maybe travel for a year or two."

Jane laid down the menu. "And this is because of Saxon?" she asked. "You two are that serious?"

Pausing, Faye gave her friend's question real consideration. Walking away from acting for a while was a new idea but something she'd been considering the last couple of days. It wasn't just because of Saxon that she wanted time outside the limelight, but she was a big part of the reason. Depending on what Saxon decided to do after this film, Faye would have to weigh her options. Still, a part of her felt the movie director would like some time off too. "We are pretty serious," Faye finally admitted. "No one's declared undying love." She laughed, trying to lighten the mood. "But..."

"But?" Jane asked with a raised eyebrow.

Faye shrugged, excitement running through her as she said the words. "I can't imagine being without her."

"But, Saxon," Courtney Mason, her manager, said, a hint of frustration creeping into her tone. They were walking across campus to the parking garage. Filming was finally over for the night. "You have your pick of some of the biggest projects in the business." Saxon shook her head. The discussion was getting tiring. For most of the evening, Courtney sat beside Saxon's chair, waiting for breaks in the action to pitch different ideas. Saxon didn't blame her for being persistent and impatient. By not answering her calls or emails, Saxon was more difficult than her manager deserved.

Slowing her steps, Saxon looked at the woman beside her. "I'm sorry," she said. "This is not fair to you, but this film has been especially challenging."

Courtney sighed. "Are you talking about Brad Norris being difficult?" she said before pausing for a beat. "Or because of something going on with Faye?"

The question brought Saxon to a stop. "Why are you asking me that?"

Stopping with her, Saxon watched Courtney search her face. "It's true then?" she asked. "You are having an affair with the lead actress of your movie?"

Saxon clenched her jaw, not wanting to lie to her manager but not happy they were having the conversation. "I like to think it is more than a movie set romance," she said. "And I would like to keep it quiet."

"Oh, Saxon," Courtney said. "You know how these things usually end. Is she why you don't want to talk about your next project?"

With her manager hitting too close to the truth, Saxon started walking again. "Call me tomorrow and we can talk," she said, leaving her frustrated manager behind. She was done talking. Faye was at her home, waiting for her.

"Talk about what?" came a voice Saxon recognized, and it was the last one she wanted to hear. Out of the shadows came the reporter who had hounded her since the start of the movie. Dressed like a student in a hoodie and jeans, with a backpack over her shoulder, she fit right in on campus. Not even bothering to acknowledge her, Saxon kept walking. Taking the key fob from her pocket, she unlocked her car, intending to get in and drive away without a conversation. The reporter didn't give up. "Hey, don't be like that. I only have one question for you." When Saxon opened her car door, the reporter grabbed hold. "Seriously, just one. Have you seen anything strange lately?" she asked. "You know, like vampires around here?"

Saxon stopped moving and turned to look at the girl. This line of questioning needed to be nipped in the bud. "Of course," she said. "*Venandi* is a vampire movie. And that's your one question." She slipped into the car seat. "Now, let go of my door."

The reporter stepped back, but a smirk still covered her face. "I think you know what I meant, Saxon Montague," she said. "I uncovered the strangest news tip yesterday. It was a few weeks old and everyone ignored the message because it sounded crazy."

Saxon forced herself to stay calm and gently closed the door. Starting the car, all she wanted was to get away from the reporter so she could think. The girl wasn't done and stepped closer to the window before making eye contact with Saxon through the glass. "It's not just the movie and you know it. Someone says you are a vampire, Saxon, and word is spreading to all the wrong people. Care to comment?"

24

LOS ANGELES, PRESENT DAY

Lifting a shimmering, red lace teddy out of her special lingerie drawer, Faye contemplated the reaction Saxon might have tonight when she wore it to bed. She liked to dress sexy for her and no longer worried about Saxon's control. Aside from the woman's sex drive being off the charts, after their first few nights together when Saxon needed taming a little, things were incredible. Finding the matching panties, she thought for a moment about Jane's comments at dinner. How she worried this might be nothing but a fling because they were shooting a movie together. A common problem in Hollywood. But then, she pushed any idea like that away. Somehow, this was different. What she felt for Saxon was beyond anything in her past, and she knew it was real. Something that would last.

Putting the teddy and panties in her overnight bag along with a few changes of clothes, she was just zipping it when the gate monitor buzzed in the kitchen. Saxon had arrived to pick her up, and with an expectant smile on her face, she carried her suitcase through the house to push the button that opened the gate. As much as she loved her house in

Beverly Hills, Malibu proved to be much more charming. Saxon's view was to die for and falling asleep to the sound of the waves felt magical. Plus, she had grown fond of Louis, and Faye looked forward to the next three days.

After grabbing her coat out of the closet, she opened the front door, surprised to see a different car than Saxon's in her driveway. This one was a black sedan and had the word 'security' written on the side. In the brightness of the motion detector light over the door, Faye had to squint to see the security guard coming toward her. "Has something happened?" she asked, alarm spreading through her. The stalker hadn't made a move in weeks, and she hoped he was no longer a problem, but if security was here then something was wrong.

"There's been a report, ma'am," the guard said as he drew nearer, and something about the tone of his voice gave Faye pause. The man's face wasn't at all familiar, and as he neared, he looked quite ordinary. Still, the sound did ring a bell, but she couldn't quite place who the guard sounded like. Then as he reached her. It clicked—the stalker. Back peddling away from the door, she tried to slam it but was too slow. With his combat boot, the attacker blocked the doorframe and pushed in quickly. Faye turned and ran to the kitchen, the man following. Before he could reach her, she slammed her hand down on the panic button and prayed help would come fast enough.

"Stay back," Faye said as she circled around the island. "Police are on the way."

Glancing at the button flashing red, the stalker let out a curse. "Then we better hurry," he said, lunging for her. Faye almost darted away from his grasp, but he caught her hair in his gloved fist. With a yank, he pulled her back against him. Faye let out a scream. This could not be happening, yet when his hand clamped over her mouth and he hissed in her ear, she was trapped.

"No one can hear you back here away from the road," he said, his breath hot on her cheek bringing back every memory from his last attack. "But you went and spoiled everything by pressing that alarm." He started to walk her forward with his body's weight against her back. "So, we will just have to go to my place."

Saxon was furious, working hard to keep her temper under control. After ignoring the reporter's questions, she had roared out of the parking lot and left campus. She should have known the pesky reporter who seemed set on digging into her life would get ahold of that tip. Everyone else disregarded it as ridiculous, but not that one, and although Saxon knew there wasn't any sort of proof, she was still concerned. Rumors had a way of taking on a life of their own in the entertainment business, and the reporter clearly implied that was happening. She and Faye needed to talk. It might be time for Saxon to disappear again, and the thought of leaving Faye behind tore her up inside. Leaving tonight would destroy everything.

Pulling up to the gate, Saxon rolled down her window to press the buzzer to let Faye know she arrived. As she reached out the window, a woman's distant scream made her freeze. The sound was so faint that only a vampire could have heard it coming from beyond the walls. It was Faye. Saxon jumped out of her car and ran toward the eight-foot security gate, effortlessly leaping over it to race up the driveway. As she got closer, the scent of the stalker came to her on the wind and made her fury rise. The man dared to try to hurt Faye again, and it would be his last mistake. Coming to

<figure>164</figure>

the top of the driveway, she saw a man dressed in a security guard's uniform dragging Faye out of her house by her hair. He was steps from the open door of a waiting sedan.

With a growl, Saxon closed in on the car. "Stop," she said, and the attacker's head snapped in her direction. Clearly, he remembered Saxon well because his eyes widened while he pushed Faye hard to the ground.

"You again," he said, reaching for the gun on his belt and leveling the weapon at Saxon. "One more step, you freak, and I'll shoot you."

With a grin, Saxon didn't resist the change this time, relishing the blast of power the release brought with it. Her eyes blazed red while her fangs grew long. Every bit of her surged with energy. This time there was no knife at Faye's throat, and the stalker would not be getting away. "So shoot," she hissed, walking toward him to close the distance.

Starting to back away, the stalker's hand holding the gun shook. "Fuck me," he said. "You are real." Then, he fired. Once. Twice. The bark of the gun was loud in the night air, and Faye screamed as the bullets hit Saxon in the middle of her chest. Reeling from the impact for a moment, Saxon almost fell but then recovered. Her grin widened, showing the white of her fangs against red lips.

"I'm so very real," she growled, moving toward him even faster. "And bullets can't kill me." In his fear, the stalker stumbled, and the gun skittered across the pavement. Reaching in his coat, the man fumbled with something Saxon couldn't see, but it didn't matter because he was about to die. At the last second, on his knees and slobbering with fear, he pulled out a set of rosary beads to try and ward her off.

"Stay away," he warned when Saxon paused. Even though the religious object did not nearly hold the power of a silver cross, she still felt pain. But not enough to stop her tonight, and she easily slapped the thing out of his hands. "No." The man begged. "Please." Saxon hissed as she bore down on him, and when he fell back onto his ass to crawl away, she watched a dark spot of urine spread down the front of his pants. Saxon chuckled, feasting on his fear, and moved to strike.

Watching from the doorway in horror, Faye knew Saxon would tear the stalker from limb to limb. As much as she hated the man, his gory death would be impossible to explain. In the distance the sound of sirens approached, and Faye knew they did not have much time. The security company she hired had a code to open the gate, meaning they would come flooding up the driveway at any minute. If they saw Saxon as a vampire, certainly all hell would break loose.

Climbing to her feet, Faye ran into the house, hoping she was fast enough. She needed a thing in a box on her fireplace mantel, and with shaking fingers, she fished it out. She hated what she was about to do, but there was no choice. While putting on the cross Louis gave her, she heard her stalker begging for his life. It was now or never if she was going to stop Saxon. Stepping out of the house, she saw Saxon flinch. With her blazing red eyes, she turned toward Faye. "Leave him," Faye said, looking directly at Saxon as she walked closer to pick up the gun off the pavement. Saxon growled, but with her every step shrank back. Faye pointed the weapon at the quivering mess of a man on the ground. "The police are coming." Saxon continued to stare at her, not looking particularly cooperative. "Change back."

"It's not that easy," Saxon growled. "I want to destroy him for hurting you."

Faye shook her head as she walked away from the front door but keeping Saxon well at bay. "I know," she said. "But you can't. Not like this. Please, just go in the house." With a final hiss, Saxon turned away from the man on the ground, and Faye noticed the two bullet holes in her clothing. "And find a different shirt. Hurry."

Skirting Faye and her necklace, Saxon ducked into the house just as two guards appeared in the driveway with guns drawn. "Freeze," the closest security guard yelled. "Nobody moves."

Still on the ground, the stalker started to point at the house. "Watch out," the man yelled, hysteria in his voice. "There's a vampire in there."

The guard started to look confused. "What the hell is going on here?" the second one said, then pointed at Faye. "Put down your weapon. Now!"

Faye lowered the gun to the ground and set it on the pavement before raising her arms to show her hands were empty. "The man on the ground has been stalking me and he tried to kidnap me tonight," she said. "He's crazy."

The two guards spread apart and the closest one picked up the gun. "You're Faye Stapleton, right? The one who sent in the emergency call?"

"Yes," she answered, grateful they were making headway as to who did what, although the security guard still seemed edgy.

"There's a vampire in the house," the stalker continued to profess over and over.

The security guard looked at Faye. "Is there someone else in the house?"

Hoping she wasn't making the mistake of her life, she

nodded. "Saxon Montague, the director of the movie I'm in. She arrived just in time to save me."

At her name, Faye watched Saxon come out the front door. Their eyes met, and a flicker of red was still in them, but then snuffed out as they drifted to look at the guard. "We were supposed to go out to dinner and talk about our final scenes," Saxon said. "I came up here when I heard her scream." That's my car down beside the gate.

"Don't listen to her," the stalker said as the second guard drug him to his feet. "That one came up here to hunt me." The man looked between the two cops to make sure he had their attention. "I'm telling you, look under her shirt. I shot her. She should be dead."

The security guard beside Faye looked from the man to Saxon. "Did he shoot you?" he asked, looking more and more confused.

Saxon shook her head. "He shot at me," she said. "But he missed. Then I tackled him while Faye got his gun."

"She's lying," the stalker exclaimed while the guard turned him around to put the handcuffs on. "She's a vampire. Look under her shirt. I shot her. You gotta listen to me."

Faye watched the security guard deliberate over what to do next. For a second, Faye thought the man beside her was going to ask Saxon to open her shirt, and she held her breath. Then, his radio squawked asking about the situation. With a last slightly suspicious glance at Saxon, he stepped away to answer the call.

25

"You really want to get out here?" the cab driver asked when Susan asked him to stop. He shook his head, clearly questioning the request. "Lady, this is no place you should be after dark. Let me take you over to the east side of the park."

Saxon leaned over the seat and handed the man money for the fare. "Thank you, but we are fine." She could understand his concern considering they had stopped on 59th street at Central Park's southern edge. All the entertainment tonight was around a little building called The Casino inside the east entrance, but that kind of action was not what they wanted. They needed a quiet, less traveled trail. What the driver didn't need to know was this area was familiar to them. On Friday nights, when the situation at the 300 Club wasn't ideal, they would come here to hunt. The routine was simple enough. At this time of night, vagrants and muggers roamed the trails waiting for naive strollers to come along. Saxon and Susan were always an unpleasant surprise for them.

"Maybe walk toward the pond again tonight?" Susan

suggested as she stepped out of the taxi and put her arm through Saxon's. Saxon smiled. Those were some of her favorite paths and she liked the view of the pond's dark water off the stone bridge. Plus, they were far enough from any electric streetlights that shadows obscured the walkways, making it unlikely they would cross paths with any casual couples strolling along. Romantic pairs weren't who they were looking for, but rather a nobody. Someone who could go to the police later after they woke up if they wanted to, but not be believable. A person they would write off as a drunk or crazy.

"The pond is a perfect choice," Saxon said as they started down the first wide, packed dirt path. "What shall we talk about tonight?" The tradition was to chat as they walked to alert any would-be attackers of their presence. Ideally, they would look like two handsomely dressed targets chitchatting along and easy to rob.

Susan pursed her lips in thought. "Maybe we should discuss moving again."

"Move?" Saxon said, caught completely off guard. "But we've hardly been here." Typically, they would settle in a large city for a few years at least, unless traveling to Europe or the Mediterranean for a pleasure trip. New York City had been their home for barely six months, and to be honest, this stop was becoming Saxon's favorite so far.

Susan gave Saxon's arm a squeeze. "I know, darling," she said. "This place is fun. Perhaps too much and people are noticing." They walked along in silence for a few minutes as Saxon contemplated the idea they might be leaving soon. She would miss the bright lights and energy of New York City.

"Where would you like to try next?" Saxon finally asked, willing to do whatever Susan wanted. She loved her, always wanting to make her happy, and perhaps they would come back to New York City someday. Time was irrelevant. Susan seemed hesitant to answer, and for a moment, Saxon wondered if there wasn't something more to her wanting to leave the big city so soon. This was more spur of the moment than the woman was putting on, especially considering she rarely did anything without proper consideration. "Susan, is something wrong?"

Pulling them to a stop, Susan turned and put a hand on her cheek. "Everything is lovely," she whispered. "You truly have been my favorite." Then, she touched her lips to Saxon's. Unlike so many of their passionate kisses, this one was light as a feather. Nothing but a whisper across her lips.

Saxon paused, looking into Susan's eyes. "I love you," she said. "But I don't understand what is going on. Did I do something?"

"Oh, never," Susan said with a tiny laugh as she started them walking toward the pond again. It was not far ahead. "But we definitely need to make this our last night. I'd like us gone by tomorrow."

Shaking her head, Saxon was entirely confused until her mind suddenly went to the man in the club. Dressed in a black suit and hat, with a silver cross around his neck, he was somehow frightening in a way Saxon couldn't quite put her finger on. Susan had acted oddly since Saxon described him and what he had said. Trying to make sense of everything in her head, she let Susan guide them to the stone bridge and up the slope to the top. From under the nearly leafless trees, the moon was brighter than it had been all night, and Saxon saw the shining orb reflected in the dark water below. Susan leaned her head against Saxon's shoulder, and Saxon relished their closeness. Still, she needed more answers. "Is this about the man I described? The one in the club?" she asked, her voice low, respecting the stillness of the night.

"Yes," Susan answered, lifting her head. "I don't like what you said about him, so we will just disappear." She looked at Saxon and smiled. In an instant, her once bright green eyes were red, and the moonlight glinted off her white fangs. "But tonight, we need to keep hunting. It's been too many days, and I don't want to be weak for our journey."

Returning her smile with fangs of her own, Saxon was ready to follow her lead. Yet, as she looked into her beautiful face, Susan's smile faltered. She let out a small cry of pain and Saxon reached for her. Confused, Saxon suddenly felt repulsed and had to fight to keep from recoiling from the woman she loved. Then, she saw it. The moonlight glinting off the silver tip of a crossbow bolt in Susan's chest. "What's happening?" Saxon groaned, fighting the force of the silver to repel her as Susan started to slide toward the ground. "Susan, no."

"Vampire hunter," Susan whispered while Saxon caught her in her arms. "I should have told you. Run." Just then, a second crossbow bolt flew past Saxon's hip and ricocheted off the stones of the bridge. Looking in the direction the thing came from, she saw the man from the speakeasy stepping out of the shadows. Saxon realized he followed their taxi here and knew what paths they might take because they did the same thing too often. Worst of all, he wore the same silver cross around his neck but held an empty crossbow in his hands. A broad smile creased his ugly face.

"I wasn't sure you both were," he chuckled, his merriment at catching them tonight clear in his laugh. "But then she was nice enough to change for me."

Fury, like she'd never felt before, shook Saxon. Standing on the bridge, she wanted to charge the man who dared attack them, but she was unwilling to let go of Susan else she fall. Even as the silver in Susan made every muscle in Saxon's body quiver, she would not let her go. "I will tear you to pieces," Saxon roared as the man moved closer. "They won't even be able to recognize you."

Although his grin disappeared, the hunter continued to walk toward the bridge while meticulously loading his weapon. Seeing the danger while Susan continued to sag in her grip, Saxon realized this may be her end. A sense of acceptance settled over Saxon. If Susan was gone, Saxon did not want to live without her. "Well, you're certainly making this easy for me," the man said as he drew closer. His smile returned and righteousness shown in his eyes as he raised the crossbow. "Go back to hell where you belong."

Without warning, Susan moved, and before Saxon could hold her back, she threw herself at the hunter. The hunter fired and the silver bolt from the weapon hit her but was not enough to stop the force of her momentum. Together they rolled back down the slope of the bridge with Susan screaming in pain and fury until they stopped in a heap. "Susan," Saxon yelled, running down the bridge, only to see the hunter push to his feet and reach for the fallen weapon.

"Stop," he commanded, patting his chest to raise the cross there. Only it wasn't. A look of shock crossed his face, followed by panic. Not hesitating, Saxon leaped on him. He tried to ward her off with his arms, but she easily pushed past his defense and grabbed him by the throat. He struggled and slapped at her hands, but he was no match for her strength as she pushed him to his knees.

"I should turn you," Saxon growled. "Make you what you hate." The man choked and struggled, but he was helpless in her grasp. "But then I would be responsible for you..."

"Saxon," she heard Susan whisper from behind her. Suddenly, the hunter meant nothing to her. He was evil and deserved no mercy. Only Susan mattered, and she tore his head from his body before letting him collapse to the ground. Rushing to Susan, she found her lying on her back, staring up at the dark sky. Forcing herself to stay at her side even though agony rippled through her body, Saxon saw the vampire hunter's silver cross in Susan's hands. The relic burned her flesh and made Susan shake with pain.

Unable to stand seeing her suffering and not caring what it did, Saxon knocked the cross from Susan's hands. Unbelievable pain shot through her and Saxon turned to vomit while the thing landed ten feet away. Yet, Saxon could see it was not enough. Susan's body still writhed in pain. Looking at her lover's chest, she could only see one of the silver tips from crossbow bolts. The other was buried deep inside. Feeling helpless and afraid, Saxon howled like an animal in great pain, and all the other creatures in the park went silent.

"Saxon." Susan reached for her, and ignoring her own pain, Saxon pulled her onto her lap.

"Susan, please," Saxon begged. "Tell me what to do."

Susan shook her head. "I'm so sorry, darling. I was selfish. Please forgive me."

"Don't say that," Saxon whispered. "You are everything. I don't want to go on without you." Susan shook her head and looked into Saxon's eyes. She opened her mouth to say something more, but before any words came out, she arched her back in pain. With a final scream, the vampire named Susan turned to dust in Saxon's hands.

26

LOS ANGELES, PRESENT DAY

S adness filled Saxon as she dropped the newspaper on the counter in Faye's kitchen. Her worst nightmare was coming true. The headline splashing across the Los Angeles Times entertainment section read 'Who is Saxon Montague?" The byline was a woman's name, and she guessed it was the reporter who kept hounding her. What was worse was the artist's sketch of her, somehow captured on the set while she sat in her director's chair.

"Unbelievable," was all Saxon could think to murmur. As she scanned the story, there was no direct reference to being a vampire or why there were no photographs of her. Clearly, the woman wasn't ready to go that far. Still, there was plenty of inference that Saxon was a fraud and needed to be investigated. Gritting her teeth in frustration, Saxon hated what it meant. She would simply have to disappear again and the thought of it was agony inside her. Leaving Faye might be too much to take. The woman was so special to her, maybe too special.

"You can sue her," Faye said as she put her hands on Saxon's shoulders to turn her away from the paper. "Celebri-

175

ties are forced to do it more than you realize. My agent will find us the best attorney."

Saxon put her hands on Faye's hips and pulled her closer to give her a light kiss. "That won't solve this," she whispered, trying to find words to explain. "I made a mistake coming to Hollywood. Dealing with the paparazzi and nosy reporters never crossed my mind." It was true. There had never been a place where she hid so much. Too many people in Los Angeles wanted to take pictures of her or know about her past. "The only good thing that's come of this was meeting you." Sadness threatened to overwhelm her, but she knew what she had to do next.

She watched Faye search her face and understanding dawned in her eyes. "Oh no," Faye said before Saxon could say another word. She clasped her shirt. "Don't say it like that."

"Faye—," Saxon started, but she clearly would have none of it and pushed away from her, hurt and anger snapping in her eyes.

She was shaking her head, but a hint of tears threatened too. "We are not over. You can't just disappear again," she said. "It's too late for that."

Saxon frowned at what she said. "Too late?"

Faye folded her arms. "Yes," she said. "This is not like your other careers. The media will not let this go if we simply disappear before finishing the movie."

Saxon did not miss the word 'we' in her statement. As much as she wanted to be with her, what Faye was inferring could not happen. She would never let Faye throw away her life in Los Angeles. Not for her. Hating how she was hurting Faye and herself, Saxon knew this was the time to go. Louis would not doubt have guessed what she would do when he read the papers this morning. He was unquestionably preparing. Stepping closer to Faye, she reached for her, wanting to somehow tell her all she meant since they met. "Please, Faye, I have to go," she said. "You don't understand. People worse than the media will come for me."

Faye continued to resist. "Don't you see? If you run it's like an admission of guilt," she said. "Finish the movie. Three days is all that is left. Please." Saxon paused, thinking over what she said, and a part of her believed Faye's advice was right. The reporter might not give up. Yet, there would be risks if she stayed. Word was out she was here, but Faye meant enough to her to stay. After all, three days might be safe enough.

The ashes glowed brightly in places in the fading daylight, but the special effects team made sure Faye had on special boots. As Agent Kolchak, she was searching what remained of the house where the vampire had been hiding. Her character used holy water to trap him and then fire to destroy the monster. The scene had been quite dramatic and required stunt doubles plus a pyrotechnics team. It all made for a great ending, although Brad Norris still pouted over it when Saxon wouldn't compromise. The only thing that remained was for Faye to say her parting lines to the LAPD detective beside her and then walk away. Off to hunt more vampires.

Looking over, she saw Saxon beside the cameraman, ready to give the signal to roll film. She looked as confident and sexy as when Faye first saw her, and she wanted her just as much. The last three days were tough while they debated what Saxon should do next. Even though she refused to listen to any talk about Faye disappearing with her, she was not giving up. She wanted to be with her and, in her heart, believed Saxon wanted the same. Vampire or not, Faye was falling in love with her.

Thankfully, everything had been quiet in the media. There were only a few halfhearted attempts by paparazzi to get onto the closed set. Ideally, interest in *Venandi* after it wrapped and started into post-production would diminish temporarily. Not until the time came to promote the movie would they have to worry. Even then, it didn't mean Saxon had to leave town. Faye still advocated for Saxon to simply lay low for a few months and let things blow over. She wanted her in Los Angeles because, by contract, Faye needed to help with the film's promotion. There were interviews to do and she had to attend the premiere. Of course, Saxon didn't have those stipulations in her contract. In fact, by reputation, she never attended anything. What mattered most though, was they would be together.

The first assistant director pointed at Faye. "Are you ready, Ms. Stapleton?" he asked, bringing her back to the moment.

She nodded. "Yes," she said. "Let's nail this." The man smiled. Her words were everyone's sentiment. One final perfect take and the filming would wrap. Taking a deep breath and focusing on the detective with her in the scene, she heard Saxon say 'action' and began. As she delivered the lines, Faye felt they were exactly what fit the moment. She said her good-bye and then turned away from the camera to leave, waiting for the word 'cut' but when it didn't come, she wasn't sure what to do. Even after she passed her mark to stop or else leave frame, there was nothing from Saxon. Something was wrong, and knowing she was off-camera, Faye whirled around to look. Saxon was still in her chair but distracted by something off to her left. So much so, she didn't even know the movie was a wrap. Following her gaze,

Faye felt her heart stop when she saw a man in a black suit standing in the road. He was grinning.

"Cut," the first assistant director said and then followed Saxon's gaze like everyone else but were too late. The man ducked into the car beside him, only to drive away.

"Who was that? It was one of them, wasn't it?" Faye asked as she paced Saxon's living room. Saxon let her talk. The woman was frightened, although she wasn't in danger. The vampire hunter didn't care about Faye and he most likely wouldn't attack if there were too many witnesses. Faye would be safe if she stayed away but insisted on coming home with her after the wrap up tonight. It was the last thing Saxon wanted because it would just make things harder. Saxon needed to go. Louis had everything ready for them.

Stepping into Faye's path, she took her hands. "Yes, he was a vampire hunter coming for me," she said, trying to keep her voice calm for Faye's sake. "Which is why I am leaving. Tonight."

She watched as Faye blinked, registering her words. "Tonight?" she repeated. "But I can't—"

"I know," Saxon interrupted. "Which is why I'm having Louis take you home. When he returns, the two of us will leave without a trace." Tears welled up in Faye's eyes, and it took everything in Saxon to resist giving in.

Faye shook her head and tried to pull away from Saxon's grip, but she held on. "No," Faye said. "No, there has to be another answer."

"There's not," Saxon said, pulling her closer to wrap her arms around the still reluctant Faye. "Please don't make this any harder."

Faye started to cry. "But I can't lose you," she said. "I am in love with you."

Her words nearly crushed Saxon with sadness. In a special way, she loved Faye too. More than anyone since Susan, and if things were different, she could see them trying to build a life together. But it was impossible in Los Angeles and she would not ask Faye to give up everything. All she could do in answer was kiss Faye, first tender and then with more passion. Their chemistry was as strong as the first moment they met.

Louis cleared his throat from the doorway. From their history, she knew he was aware of the danger. "I'm sorry," he said. "But the car's ready." Saxon stepped back with those words, and although Faye continued to shake her head, she stepped back too.

"Please tell me you will contact me and let me know you are safe," she said, tears streaming down her cheeks. "And this is not good-bye, Saxon Montague."

Feeling more grief than she expected, all Saxon could do was nod. "I will reach out to you," Louis explained from the doorway. "I promise. But we need to hurry. For Saxon's safety." Those words seem to help Faye gather herself and, with a last lingering look, turned to follow Louis out the front door. As she heard the door close, Saxon walked to the sliding glass windows that looked out over the ocean.

Even though moving here turned out to be a mistake, there were so many things she was going to miss. The view was one of them. She loved the sound of the waves as they calmed her on restless nights. A partial moon was out, and she was reminded of the stroll she took with Faye not long ago and felt a yearning to go down to the beach. If nothing but to touch her toes in the cool sand. She had a few minutes before Louis came back.

Making up her mind to go, she slipped out the glass doors and took the stairs down. The night was quiet, but for the crash of the ocean, and as she slipped off her shoes and socks, she was thankful for the solitude. The other houses to the left and right were dark as she started to walk. Letting her mind wander, she thought of Susan and that first night in New Orleans. She never loved anyone more, and after she lost her, things were never the same. Yet Faye gave her pause. Saxon realized the woman made her happy. Maybe there would be a way for them. Somehow.

"Midnight stroll?" came a man's voice over the wind and the sound of the waves. Saxon knew who was speaking before she even glanced over her shoulder in the direction of the house. The vampire hunter she saw earlier followed her with a silver cross around his neck and a crossbow in his hands. It was stupid to think the man wouldn't have followed her here. Perhaps a part of her wanted this.

With resignation, she stopped and felt the waves off his silver cross battering her. In a moment, her ashes would be blowing with the wind across the ocean. "What are you waiting for?" she growled, but before the man could reply, a gunshot rang out. Saxon winced, thinking she was the target, but felt nothing and, after a moment, turned. The vampire hunter lay face down, covering his cross with his body while blood from his head made the sand darker in the moonlight. Confused, Saxon looked around for the shooter. Out of the darkness walked a woman that Saxon instantly recognized. The reporter who wouldn't leave her alone.

Saxon looked from the dead man to the reporter and back. "How...?" she started but wasn't even sure what to ask.

"I honestly didn't think he would be lured out before you disappeared again," the reporter said, putting the gun back in her shoulder bag. "I mean, seriously, how many more clues that you are a vampire did I have to leave."

Saxon shook her head. "What are you talking about?" she asked, and the reporter smiled a moment before changing into a vampire herself. Stunned, all Saxon could do was blink.

"Surprised, I see," she said, her eyes glowing red and the fangs in her mouth bright white in the moonlight. "I wasn't sure about you either, hence the constant questions. Sorry to end up using you as bait, Saxon." She kicked the dead man's foot. "But I've been trying to kill this one for years."

"You hunt the hunters," she murmured, finally understanding. "And once you knew I was the vampire you were looking for, used me to get him."

The reporter turned back to normal and nodded. "Yes," she said. "And it's time to let this one wash out to sea while we both get out of town." She started back toward Saxon's house. "There will be others and I might not see them in time."

27

BANGKOK, THREE MONTHS LATER

As the airplane captain announced to the passengers that they would be landing soon, Faye closed her eyes and relaxed in her seat. The last three months were a whirlwind, and she was looking forward to a break. She testified against her stalker, who had targeted many women, and so remained behind bars. With that behind her, she spent the rest of her time fulfilling her promises to her agent by helping promote *Venandi*. All her hard work had paid off. The movie was a hit with the public and the early reviews from critics leaned toward favorable. Faye's name was already coming up in conversations about award contention. Movie viewers thankfully accepted her outside her typical character, and Walt was already reaching out to her with more serious roles.

That could all wait, though. Through Louis, Faye kept in minimal contact with Saxon. It was hard and a minute didn't pass that Faye didn't think of Saxon. Finally, she would see her again. To ensure she wasn't followed, the location where she would land was kept a secret. Louis made all the arrangements and Faye only found out when she arrived at

KC LUCK

the airport to pick up the tickets. Bangkok, the capital of Thailand.

Looking out her window, she saw the lights of the city bright against the dark below. Arriving in the middle of the night, she hoped Saxon would be there to greet her. The thought of the woman made her heart quicken. To look into her dark eyes, kiss her full lips, and hold her again was all Faye wanted. There was no return ticket, and she had no immediate intention to return to Los Angeles. Right now, all she wanted was to be with Saxon.

Saxon rode in the taxi through Bangkok's dark streets. Traffic was still heavy even though it was the middle of the night, but they would get to the airport soon enough. Louis wanted to pick up Faye, but Saxon insisted. If anyone was going to meet Faye, she wanted to be the one. For the last three months, Faye was always on her mind–their chemistry and how good they seemed to fit. There was also Faye's acceptance of Saxon, so everything should be perfect, but still Saxon hesitated.

As much as she loved Faye, and she believed she did, it made her question if she was doing the right thing. A life with a vampire who never aged and was forever moving from place to place didn't seem fair to ask of her. Faye would never be able to tell the world who she loved. Internationally famous, she would always have to stay under the radar, which might prove impossible. Especially since publicity was part of her lifelong career. Saxon could not ignore the facts. What she asked of Faye was selfish and unfair, yet a life without her would continue to be lonely. Louis kept telling her she could love again, but Saxon wasn't sure. With a sigh, she leaned forward and knocked on the window

184

between her and the cab driver. Quickly, she gave him new directions. It was time to follow her instincts and make a decision.

Walking through the airport with a porter behind her pushing her three suitcases on a cart, the nighttime humidity was thick, and she wasn't even outside yet. Ahead were the sliding glass doors that would lead outside and where she hoped someone was waiting for her. She doubted a driver would be sent as that would require holding a sign with her name on it. Wearing a big hat and sunglasses, even though it was night, she was working hard to stay unrecognizable. So, if not a driver, then that left either Saxon or Louis waiting for her. The idea of possibly seeing Saxon in only moments was nearly too much to stand.

Before she made the door, her cellphone started buzzing in her pocket. With not many people knowing the new number and considering the time it was back in Los Angeles, she thought the call might be from Louis. Pulling the thing out to look at the screen, she saw she had guessed correct. Furrowing her brow, she hoped everything was alright and answered without missing a step. Perhaps he was checking on her status, and any second, she would see him waiting for her.

"Hello," she said. "Is everything okay?"

There was a pause and anxiety rolled in Faye's stomach. Something was wrong. She could feel it. Then, the thought came to her. Saxon didn't want to meet her after all. "Faye," Louis started, but she was not sure she could stand what he was going to say next. This could not be happening, and then she was on the sidewalk to see for herself. A group of drivers held signs with names. Family members were there to greet people coming out. Cab drivers called out to offer a ride. But no Louis, and even worse, no Saxon. Looking right and left, she stood stunned as people milled around her.

Then, she felt a presence beside her. "Looking for someone?" the person said. Turning to look, Saxon stood with a bouquet of flowers in her hand and a smile on her gorgeous face.

Tears of happiness springing to her eyes, Faye felt all her fears slip away. The woman she loved was here for her. "Yes, I am," she said. "Looking for you."

THE END

Want more?
Sign up for my newsletter (http://eepurl.com/dx_iEf) to keep tabs on what I am writing next.

ABOUT THE AUTHOR

Bestselling author KC Luck writes action adventure, contemporary romance, and lesbian fiction. Writing is her passion, and nothing energizes her more than creating new characters facing trials and tribulations in a complex plot. Whether it is apocalypse, horror, or a little naughty, with every story, KC tries to add her own unique twist. She has written eleven books (which include *The Darkness Trilogy* and *The Lesbian Billionaires Club* series) and multiple short stories across many genres. KC is active in the f/f community and is a member of the GLCS board of directors.

To receive updates on KC Luck's books, please consider subscribing to her mailing list (http://eepurl.com/dx_iEf). Also, KC Luck is always thrilled to hear from her readers (kc. luck.author@gmail.com)

To follow KC Luck, you can find her at:
Website – www.kc-luck.com
Amazon Author Page - https://www.amazon.com/KC-Luck/e/B07BK5ZRYT

facebook.com/kc.luckauthor.92
instagram.com/kc_luckauthor

AFTERWORD

Enjoy this book?
You can make a big difference

Honest reviews of my books help bring them to the attention of other readers. If you've enjoyed this story, I would be incredibly grateful if you could spend a couple minutes leaving a review (it can be as short as you like) on the book's Amazon and Goodreads pages.

ALSO BY KC LUCK

Rescue Her Heart

Save Her Heart

Welcome to Ruby's

Back to Ruby's

Darkness Falls

Darkness Remains

Darkness United

The Lesbian Billionaires Club

The Lesbian Billionaires Seduction

The Lesbian Billionaires Last Hope

Made in the USA
Coppell, TX
29 March 2021

52417210R00114